"This is not wise."

His eyes moved almost compulsively to her mouth, and she realized he was as aware of what was happening as she was.

"Then let me go," she pleaded unsteadily, though she made no attempt to move away.

And Enrique sensed that she was susceptible to this sudden intimacy between them. It was evident in the dark fire that blazed suddenly in his eyes.

"I will," he said savagely, but his actions belied his words. His head dipped until his lips were only a few inches away from hers. "I must," he added barely audibly, before he bent even lower and touched her mouth with his.

VIVA LA VIDA DE AMOR!

They speak the language of passion.

In Harlequin Presents®, you'll find a
special kind of lover—full of Latin charm.
Whether he's relaxing in jeans, or dressed
for dinner, giving you diamonds, or
simply sweet dreams, he's got spirit,
style and sex appeal!

Latin Lovers is the miniseries
from Harlequin Presents® for anyone
who's passionate about love and life.

Anne Mather

THE SPANIARD'S SEDUCTION

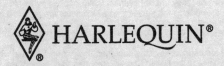

HARLEQUIN®

TORONTO • NEW YORK • LONDON
AMSTERDAM • PARIS • SYDNEY • HAMBURG
STOCKHOLM • ATHENS • TOKYO • MILAN • MADRID
PRAGUE • WARSAW • BUDAPEST • AUCKLAND

ISBN 0-373-12248-9

THE SPANIARD'S SEDUCTION

First North American Publication 2002.

Copyright © 2002 by Anne Mather.

CHAPTER ONE

IT HAD rained in the night, and when Enrique stepped out onto his balcony at six o'clock the morning air brought a feathering of goosebumps over his flesh.

Of course it was very early, too early for the pale thread of the rising sun to give any warmth to the day. He should still be in his bed—or rather in Sanchia's bed, as she had expected—instead of standing here, brooding over something that alone could bring an unwelcome thinning of his blood.

His long fingers curled impatiently over the iron railing. It was still much warmer here, even at this ungodly hour of the morning, than it had been in England, he recalled, not altogether wisely. Despite the fact that early June in Andalusia meant blue skies and long days of hot sunshine, London had been cool and overcast while he was there, making him glad to be boarding the plane to come back home.

Only to find *that* letter waiting for him…

He scowled. He didn't want to think about that now. He'd spent far too many hours thinking about it already and it was all too easy to allow his anger to overtake his common sense. The realisation that, if his father hadn't been so ill, the letter would have been delivered to him filled him with outrage. It was only because Julio de Montoya was in the hospital in Seville that the letter had lain unopened on his desk until Enrique's return the day before.

His hands tightened on the railing, his fingertips brushing the petals of the morning glory that climbed the pillars beneath his balcony. Raindrops sparkled, creating a rainbow of colour on the pearly-white blossoms, drawing his eyes lower to where a veritable waterfall of jasmine and bougainvillaea spilled their beauty in the courtyard below.

Enrique had always believed his home was the most beautiful place on earth, but this morning it was difficult to empty his mind of intrusive thoughts, destructive thoughts. Even the sunlight glinting on the spire of the church in the valley below the *palacio* brought him no pleasure today, and he turned back into his apartments with a barely controlled feeling of frustration.

The letter was lying on the floor beside his bed, thrown there after he had read it for the umpteenth time at three o'clock that morning, but he ignored it. Even though the temptation was to pick it up and read it once again, he put the impulse aside and, stripping off the silk boxers which were all he wore to sleep in, he strode into the adjoining bathroom.

He ran the shower hot at first, using its pummelling spray to warm his chilled flesh. Then, after thoroughly cleansing his hair and body, he turned the thermostat to cold. The shock of the ice-cold water sharpened his senses, and, feeling more ready to face the day, he turned off the taps and stepped out.

A pile of towels were stacked on a rack beside the shower cubicle and Enrique wrapped one about his hips before taking another to dry his straight black hair. His jaw was rough, evidence of the night's growth of beard, and, slotting a towel about his neck, he studied his reflection in the mirror above the handbasin with a critical eye.

He looked as rough as his jawline, he thought grimly, scraping a hand over his chin. His olive skin had a sallow cast and his deep-set dark eyes were hollowed by the dark circles that surrounded them. Narrow cheekbones flared above thin lips that were presently set in a forbidding line, and although women seemed to find his appearance appealing he could see no attraction in his hostile face.

But then, that was what came of burning the candle at both ends, he conceded. He'd flown back from London only the previous morning, and had spent the afternoon in meetings that would have been exhausting at the best of times. Then Sanchia had expected him to spend the evening with her; more than the evening, as it had turned out. Though much to her disappointment he had declined. Nevertheless, it had been after two o'clock when he'd crawled into bed—but not to sleep. The letter had made sure of that, and he scowled again as he thought of it lying there, waiting for him to pick it up, waiting for him to deal with it.

And he would have to deal with it. Soon. Before his father came home from the hospital, which might be in the next few days. When he'd spoken to his mother yesterday evening, she'd been overjoyed to report that the surgery her husband had undergone had proved so successful. Now, with care and a certain amount of luck, Julio de Montoya should have several more years of active life ahead of him. That was so long as nothing untoward happened to hinder his recovery.

Like that letter.

Enrique's jaw compressed and, after smothering the lower half of his face with foam, he reached for his razor. Dammit, what did that—*bruja*—hope to achieve? And who was the child—if there really was a child—who had reputedly written the letter? No kin of his, he was sure. Or of Antonio's. Cassandra had probably invented the whole thing. So what game was she playing?

Cassandra...

His hand slipped and the razor sliced into his cheek. Swearing as blood dripped onto the towel around his neck, Enrique groped for the tap. Then, after sluicing his face with cold water, he waited for the blood to congeal. What the hell was wrong with him, he wondered, letting that letter cause him such grief? He had to get a hold of himself, and damn quick. He'd done it ten years ago and he could do it now. He had no intention of letting that woman ruin his life. Again. She might be Antonio's widow, but she had no connection with this family. None at all.

The cut had stopped bleeding by the time he'd dressed in loose cotton trousers and a black tee shirt. Deck shoes slipped easily onto his narrow feet and he used a comb on his still-damp hair. Then, despite his unwillingness to do so, he bent and picked up the letter and opened it once more.

It was only a short letter, written in a distinctly childish hand. Had Cassandra used her left hand to write it? It might explain the immature scrawl, the evident effort taken to form the letters. A child of nine could have written it, he supposed, but as he refused to accept its content he couldn't accept its validity.

The temptation to tear the letter into shreds was appealing. He doubted if even Cassandra would have the nerve to write again, and once it was destroyed he could forget all about it.

But he couldn't do it. Despite his suspicions, despite the fact that Antonio's untimely death meant he had no nieces or nephews, a sick kind of curiosity demanded to know what was at the bottom of it.

Even the paper offended his sensibilities. A single sheet of lined notepaper, the kind a stenographer might use to take notes at a meeting, or, more likely, a sheet torn from a child's notepad, just to reinforce the illusion of innocence.

Innocence!

His lips curled as he spread the page between his fingers and read again the message that had so angered him.

> *Dear Grandpa,*
> *You don't know me and Mum says you don't want to but I don't believe that. I'd like us to be friends and that's why I've got Mum to bring me to Spain on holiday this year. We're coming on June 12 and we're staying in Punta del Lobo at the Pensión del Mar. I know it's by the sea, but I don't know if it's a long way from Tuarega, but anyway you could come to see us. I'm sure Mum would like to see you whatever she says.*
> *With love from your grandson, David de Montoya.*

Enrique's teeth clenched. How dared she call her child de Montoya? he thought savagely. If indeed there was a child, he reminded himself again. But, if so, he had to be some bastard born after Antonio was dead and buried. And Enrique knew——

But that was a path he had no intention of being drawn down. Whatever he knew or didn't know about Cassandra was not in question here. His only concern was in ensuring that his father never saw the letter, never suffered the pain of knowing that once again Cassandra Scott—de Montoya, dammit—was trying to insinuate herself into his family.

His fingers curled about the cheap sheet of paper, screwing it into a tight ball in his palm. He didn't want to look at it. He never wanted to see it again. But he had the feeling that, whatever he did, nothing would erase the memory of the words.

He aimed the ball of paper at his wastebin, and then dropped his arm again. If he left the letter there, someone might be curious enough to wonder what it was and unravel it. Unless he was prepared to tear it into pieces and put it into the lavatory, or set fire to it, he would have to dispose of it elsewhere.

Which was what he would do, he decided, neither of the other alternatives having much appeal to him. He refused to consider he might have any unacknowledged motive for hanging onto the missive. It was, after all, the only evidence he had that Cassandra had tried to reach his father.

Smoothing the letter out again, he opened a drawer in his bedside cabinet and slipped it between the pages of his missal. An ironic smile touched his lips at the incongruity of its resting place, but at least he was fairly sure that no one else was likely to find it there.

That still didn't solve the problem of what he was going to do about it, he reflected later, after the maid had served him strong black coffee and warm brioche at a table set beneath the arching canopy of the colonnade. At this hour it was extremely pleasant eating breakfast outdoors, and normally this was the time of day when Enrique reviewed the work that had been done the previous day and consulted his managers' reports of work in progress. As his father's deputy—and in recent weeks the nominal head of the de Montoya corporation—Enrique took his responsibilities seriously. It was infuriating to think that this morning his thoughts were constantly bombarded by the knowledge that it was already June the fifteenth and Cassandra—and possibly her son—were only thirty miles away at Punta del Lobo.

Had the boy—if there was a boy—already found out how

far it was from Punta del Lobo to Tuarega? Was it conceivable that Cassandra might go so far as to come to the estate?

Unable to sit still with such a prospect for company, Enrique picked up his coffee and walked restlessly across the courtyard to where a stone nymph cooled her heels in the waters of the fountain. He paused beside the stone basin and tried to calm his thoughts with the sight of the cream waterlilies that floated in the pool. The *palacio* circled three sides of this central courtyard, the fourth edged with purple azalea and scarlet oleander, whose mingled perfumes found little favour with him this morning. A warm breeze blew up from the valley, tumbling the drying strands of his thick hair over his forehead, and he thrust them back with impatient fingers.

Dammit, why now? he wondered, taking an absent mouthful of his coffee. After almost ten years, why choose this time to break her silence? Was it possible she'd read about his father's illness? Did she think the old man might be more—approachable now, having been faced with his own mortality?

It was possible. Indeed, it was the only explanation that made any sense. Putting aside the unlikely premise that this boy, David de Montoya—he baulked at using that name—had written the letter, what else did he have? So what did he intend to do about it?

Cassandra stood on the sand, shading her eyes as she watched her son playing in the water. He'd made friends with a German boy who was also staying at the *pensión* and they'd spent the past couple of hours competing with each other on the plastic floats they'd hired from the beach attendant. This cove was the ideal place for children, and, although she'd had misgivings when she'd booked the holiday, there was no doubt that they were both benefiting from the break.

But it was already nearly five o'clock and Cassandra could feel her shoulders prickling in spite of the layering of sunscreen she'd applied and reapplied during the afternoon. Three days was not long enough to become completely acclimatised, and, although her skin wasn't as sensitive now as it had been when they'd arrived, she knew better than to risk getting burned.

David didn't have that problem. His skin already possessed a stronger pigment, and, even though she'd insisted on his wearing some protection, he didn't seem to be affected by the sun. Which wasn't unexpected considering his ancestry, Cassandra thought wryly. Not even nine years spent in a cool northern climate could significantly alter the pattern of heredity, and his skin was already acquiring a deeper tan.

Which she couldn't hope to emulate, she reflected, brushing the sand from her arms with slim fingers. She rarely tanned, her pale skin turning pink or red, depending on the circumstances, and then reverting to a creamy white again as soon as the heat subsided. But at least she didn't suffer the ignominy of freckles, even if her unruly mass of hair was more red than copper.

She glanced about her and noticed that the beach was emptying fast. Most people were making their way back to the hotels and *pensiónes* that dotted the hillside below the small town of Punta del Lobo, and Cassandra mimed to her son that it was time they were leaving, too. The beach was used almost exclusively by tourists and, like her, Cassandra guessed they were all looking forward to a cool shower and a change of clothes before venturing out for the evening meal.

Because of David, Cassandra ate earlier than many of their fellow guests. Europeans often had dinner at nine or even ten o'clock in the evening, but as David was invariably up at dawn, by ten o'clock Cassandra was wilting, too.

Still, it was nice to eat at one of the outdoor cafés or *tapas* bars that thronged the small square, and Cassandra looked forward to the glass of wine she usually allowed herself with the meal. Well, she was on holiday, after all, she defended herself, bending to pick up her beach bag and the towels lying on top of it. It had taken long enough, goodness knew, for her to feel sufficiently confident to make the trip.

She straightened and looked about her once again. Despite the fact that this bay was at least an hour's drive from Tuarega, she couldn't completely dispel the apprehension that gripped her when she was alone like this. This was the de Montoyas' territory, after all, and it wouldn't do to forget it.

Not that she truly expected to see anyone she knew. None of them knew they were here and she was a fool to anticipate anything unexpected happening. It would be too much of a coincidence if any member of the de Montoya family turned up in Punta del Lobo. She was worrying unnecessarily.

All the same, when David had once again broached the idea of them coming to Spain on holiday, she had demurred. She supposed he'd been six or seven years old when he'd first asked if they could go to Spain, and it had been comparatively easy at that time to find excuses not to go. This year she hadn't been able to put him off, and, telling herself that Spain was a big country, she'd given in.

She'd had second thoughts, of course, when David had chosen Andalusia, but she'd had to admit that it was one of the most attractive areas in the brochure. And, not wanting to provoke more questions, she'd swallowed her inhibitions and booked it. Despite her fears, no one at the *pensión* had questioned their identity. After all, Punta del Lobo was not Cadiz. She was sure they would be safe enough there.

Her father thought she was mad, of course. But then, Mr Scott had always maintained that she should never have told David his father had been a Spaniard. Though how could she not? she argued. His name was so distinctive. It was only now, as David got older, that she could see her father might have had a point.

But not now, please God, she mused, as her son ran up to her, spraying her with seawater. Horst was with him and Cassandra smiled at the German boy with genuine warmth. Horst's parents had gone to Seville for the day, but the boy had wanted to stay with David and Cassandra had agreed to look after him. He was a nice boy and far more biddable than her son.

No surprise there, then...

Cassandra cut herself off. She had no intention of getting into the reasons for that; no desire to remind herself of the generations of proud arrogant genes that ran in his blood. God knew, it was hard not to think about it every time she looked at him, but somehow, over the years, she had managed to subjugate all her bitterness where her son was concerned.

And she couldn't imagine life without him; that was part of the problem. The fear that one day the de Montoyas might find out she had had a son was an ever-present anxiety, but after nine years she was becoming a little less apprehensive. One day, maybe, when David was fully grown and able to make his own decisions, she might tell him who his father had been. But that was far in the future and not something she even wanted to contemplate at this moment.

'Do we have to go?'

David had picked up his towel and was rubbing it vigorously over his hair. Cassandra smiled and handed Horst his towel before replying, 'I'm afraid so. It's getting late. Haven't you noticed? We're practically the last people on the beach.'

David grimaced. 'So?' he said, arching an imperious brow, and just for a minute Cassandra was reminded of his father's ruthless face.

'So, it's time we were getting back to the *pensión*,' she declared tersely, angry with herself for putting that connotation on him. It was because they were here, because of what she had been thinking, she realised, hiding her irritation. It wasn't David's fault that she was on edge.

'It has been a good day, Mrs de Montoya,' said Horst, his precise English almost better than David's. 'It was most kind of you to let me stay.'

'No problem,' said Cassandra, jockeying her son into putting on his shorts. 'We were happy to have you, weren't we, David?'

'What? Oh, yeah.' David grinned, and he and Horst exchanged a high-handed slap. 'I like showing him what a ditz he is when it comes to board racing.'

'Ditz? What is that, a ditz?' queried Horst, and then grinned himself when he realised the joke was at his expense. 'Jerk,' he said succinctly. 'I will not tell you what I could call you if your mother was not here.'

'Feel free,' taunted David, and, giving the other boy a push, he darted off along the beach.

Horst followed him, and pretty soon they were rolling and tumbling together, with a complete disregard for the clothes they had just donned.

Cassandra sighed, and after returning the two boards the boys had left to the attendant she started after them, easily overtaking them with her long-legged stride. Her ankle-length voile skirt was showing the effects of sand and seawater, too, and she draped David's towel about her shoulders to protect her smarting shoulders as she reached the cliff path.

The boys went up ahead of her, David the taller and therefore the quicker of the two. He was already a good-looking boy and she could imagine what a heartthrob he was going to be when he was older. So long as he didn't do what his father had done, she mused sombrely. That was one problem she did not want to have to deal with again.

The Pensión del Mar was situated near the top of the cliff path, a narrow-fronted building with a striped awning protecting its pristine white façade. Cassandra had been favourably impressed with its appearance and with the service offered which, considering what they were paying, was considerably cheaper than similar accommodation back home. The proprietor, Señor Movida, was a charming man, too, and he was doing everything he could to make their stay a happy one.

To Cassandra's relief, the small Fiat that the Kaufmans had hired was parked on the gravelled forecourt of the *pensión*, which meant that Horst's parents were back. In fact, Herr Kaufman was standing in the doorway to the *pensión*, watching for his son, and Horst bounded ahead to greet his father.

'Lucky dog,' muttered David enviously, and Cassandra cast a startled look his way.

'What did you say?'

'I said Horst is lucky having a father,' declared David gruffly. Then, before his mother could make any response, 'I wonder if there's been any post for us.'

'Post?' Cassandra blinked. 'Do you mean a letter? Who

would be writing to us? We just spoke to your grandfather last night on the phone.'

David shrugged. 'I don't know,' he said, not altogether convincingly, and Cassandra knew a sudden chill. But then Herr Kaufman was coming towards them and she was forced to put her own doubts aside.

'Thank you for looking after Horst, Mrs de Montoya,' he said warmly, his eyes moving appreciatively over her slender figure so that she became intensely conscious of her damp skirt. 'Has Horst been good?'

'He's been very good,' Cassandra answered swiftly, wondering if she was only imagining the avidity of his gaze. 'Did you enjoy your trip?'

'It was most enlightening,' replied the man, nodding. 'We visited many of the palaces and museums. Not something my son would be particularly interested in, I think.'

Cassandra forced a smile. 'I think not,' she agreed. 'I can't imagine David being interested in old buildings either.'

'I might be,' protested her son, but Herr Kaufman wasn't listening to the boy.

'Did you know that your name, de Montoya, is quite a famous one in Andalusia?' he asked conversationally. 'We have been reading some literature about this area, and it seems the de Montoya family is well-known both for the quality of the fortified wines they produce and for the magnificent bulls they breed on their estate just north of here. I do not suppose you are related to them, Mrs de Montoya?'

'No,' said Cassandra quickly, aware that David was now listening to Herr Kaufman with unusual interest. She gestured towards the *pensión*. 'Is that likely?' she asked, trying to make a joke of it, and then felt the fizzy soda she had consumed in the middle of the afternoon rise into her throat.

A man had just emerged from the building behind Horst's father and she felt the colour drain out of her face. Almost convulsively, she clamped a desperate hand on David's shoulder. The boy objected, but for once she was unaware of him. Her eyes were riveted on the newcomer. It couldn't be, she thought sickly. But it was. Enrique de Montoya had paused in

the doorway of the *pensión* and was presently surveying the
scene that greeted his cold dark eyes with a mixture of satisfaction and contempt.

Dear God, how could this be? she fretted weakly. She'd
told no one but her father that she was coming here, to this
particular address. People knew she was holidaying in Spain,
of course. Her boss at the bookshop where she worked knew,
for example. She'd had to tell him what she was doing when
she'd arranged for the time off. But he wouldn't have told
anyone. No one here, anyway. Certainly not the de Montoyas.

Her mouth dried. He looked just the same, she thought painfully: just as proud, just as arrogant, just as condescending as
before. And just as attractive, though her attraction to him had
been as crazy as that of the rabbit to the snake. He'd used that
attraction, too, ruthlessly, and then expected her to do exactly
as he'd wanted.

'Is something wrong?'

Herr Kaufman had noticed her pale face and Cassandra
hoped with a desperate longing that it was only a terrible coincidence that Enrique was here. He'd seen them, but perhaps
he hadn't recognised them. Well, her actually. He'd never seen
David, didn't even know of his existence.

She had to get away. The urge to run was irresistible, and,
without considering what David might think of her sudden
change of plan, she tightened her hold on his shoulder.

'I've got a headache,' she told Herr Kaufman swiftly. 'It
must be the sun. David, come with me. I need some aspirin.
We'll just pop along to the *farmacia*—'

'Oh, Mum!' David was predictably awkward. 'Do we have
to? We've just got back from the beach. I want a shower.'

'David!'

'Perhaps I can be of some assistance,' broke in Herr
Kaufman, possibly seeing a chance to compensate her for
looking after his son. 'I'd be happy to go to the *farmacia* for
you.'

'Oh, no. I—'

But it was too late. Before she could formulate a convincing
excuse, one which would allow her to escape before Enrique

recognised them, a tall shadow fell across their little group. And a voice, one which she would have sworn she'd forgotten, cut into their exchange.

'Cassandra?' Even the way he said her name was horribly familiar. 'It is Cassandra, is it not? I am not mistaken?'

As if Enrique de Montoya would ever admit to being mistaken about anything, thought Cassandra wildly, forced to tip her head back to look up at him. He knew exactly who she was, and before she could do anything to protect her son Enrique's dark eyes had moved almost dismissively to the boy at her side.

'And this must be—David,' he continued, only to suck in a strangled breath when he saw the boy.

David! Cassandra blinked. How had he known her son's name? But before she found an answer to this, she saw the devastation his identity had wrought in Enrique's stunned expression. Yes, look at him, she wanted to scream accusingly. See what you did; see what you've lost!

But of course she didn't do anything of the kind. The de Montoyas were too polite for that. Besides, Herr Kaufman was still there, looking at Enrique with considering eyes, glancing from him to Cassandra and back again with obvious enquiry. He was probably wondering what someone who looked like Enrique de Montoya—who dressed like Enrique de Montoya—could have in common with a rather dishevelled English housewife. Enrique's three-piece suit and grey silk shirt were obviously designer-made, whereas Cassandra's clothes had never been particularly stylish, even when they were new.

'You are a friend of Mrs de Montoya?' It was the German who spoke, although David was close on his heels.

'Do you know my grandfather?' he demanded, and even as Cassandra was absorbing the shock of learning that her son knew something about this Enrique found his tongue.

'I—yes,' he said through clenched teeth, the look he cast at Cassandra full of emotions she couldn't hope to identify. 'I— I am your—' His harsh voice was strained. 'Your uncle,' he got out tightly. 'Enrique.' He took a laboured breath. 'I am—happy to meet you at last.'

'You are Enrique de Montoya? *The* Enrique de Montoya?'

Herr Kaufman was persistent, and although Cassandra could hardly blame him for being curious, she wished he would show some discretion.

Enrique was gradually recovering his composure, however. She could see it in the way he straightened his shoulders and looked at the other man with bleak assessing eyes. He'd weathered the blow she'd dealt him and now he was exercising damage control. He had no intention of allowing anyone else to see his real feelings, and his thin lips lifted in a cold smile.

'I have that privilege,' he said now, in answer to the other man's question. 'And you are?'

'Kaufman,' said the German eagerly. 'Franz Kaufman, *señor*.' He held out his hand. 'It is a great pleasure to meet you.'

Enrique hesitated long enough to make the other man uneasy before accepting the gesture. 'How do you do?' he responded, and then turned back to Cassandra.

'Are you really my uncle?'

David had been silent long enough, and at last Franz Kaufman seemed to realise he was intruding. 'If you will excuse me, Horst and I must go and see if my wife is ready to go into town,' he declared, and Cassandra saw Enrique's brow arch in acknowledgement.

He'd probably thought the other man was with her, she brooded bitterly. God, she wished he was, she thought, forgetting her own discomfort with Kaufman's familiarity earlier. But she wished she had some weapon to use against Enrique, something to hurt this man who had attempted to destroy her life.

CHAPTER TWO

THE silence after Franz Kaufman's departure was deafening. Enrique guessed it was up to him to answer the boy's question, but for all his appearance of calm he was as taut as a violin string inside.

God! He'd been so sure he knew what he was doing when he'd decided to come to the Pensión del Mar and confront Cassandra with her sordid little deception. So sure it was the only thing he could do to keep her away from his father. Instead, he was left with the distinct suspicion that he should have left well enough alone.

'I—yes,' he said, after deciding there was no point in denying their kinship. 'Antonio de Montoya was my brother,' he conceded obliquely, aware that Cassandra was looking almost as sick as he felt. 'You are David, I presume?'

Before the boy could answer, however, Cassandra grasped her son's arm and pulled him round to face her. 'What have you done?' she demanded harshly, her voice thick with emotion. 'What have you done?'

The boy had the grace to blush at his mother's obvious distress. 'I told you there might be some post for us,' he mumbled, trying to drag himself away from her. 'I didn't know— *he*—was going to turn up, did I?'

No, he hadn't known that, admitted Enrique to himself. But perhaps he should have suspected that such a bombshell would secure more than a casual response.

Unless… Unless the boy had assumed that his paternal grandfather knew of his existence?

'Did you really expect we might ignore your letter?' he asked now, supremely conscious of Cassandra standing stiffly beside her son, her whole being emitting the kind of hostility he'd never thought to have to face again. It was hard to remember that she had brought this on herself. It wasn't his fault that she'd chosen to keep her son's existence from them.

'No.' David swung round, evidently relieved to be distracted from his mother's fury. 'I knew you'd want to see me. I told Mum ages ago that I wanted to meet my Spanish grandfather, but she said you weren't interested in us.'

'Did she?' Enrique couldn't keep the bitterness out of his voice. 'But she told you how to get in touch with us, no?'

'No!' Cassandra was incensed. 'I wouldn't do such a—'

But David's excited voice overrode her protest. 'No, Mum didn't tell me anything. I got your address from my dad's passport,' he explained proudly. 'Mum keeps it in a box upstairs.' He gave his mother a defiant look as she tried to interrupt him. 'You do,' he insisted, clearly deciding he might never have another chance to defend himself. 'You know you do. Along with all that other stuff: Dad's wallet and letters and things.' He sighed ruefully. 'I'm sorry.' Although he didn't look it. 'I found the box when I was looking for—for something else.'

'What?' Cassandra's demand promised retribution, and David hunched his thin shoulders.

'My catapult,' he muttered, and she stared at him.

'You were looking for your catapult in my wardrobe?' she exclaimed scornfully. 'You expect me to believe that?'

'It's true.' David was defensive now. 'I'd already looked in your knicker drawer and—'

Cassandra uttered something unrepeatable, and despite the seriousness of the situation Enrique felt his lips twitch with uncontrollable mirth. There was something so ludicrous in talking about catapults and knicker drawers when moments before his whole life had shifted on its axis.

But his humour must have shown in his face because Cassandra turned on him, her anger dispersing any pretence of courtesy he might have made. 'You find it funny?' she demanded caustically. 'Well, of course, why would I expect anything different from you? No doubt you find the whole thing hilarious. You and your father can have a good laugh about it when you get home. Which I suggest should be sooner rather than later. Whatever you may think, there's nothing for you here.'

Enrique sobered. 'You think not?' he asked succinctly, and knew a momentary satisfaction when anxiety replaced the fury in her eyes. 'I beg to differ.'

Cassandra held up her head, and he had to admire the way she overcame her obvious dismay. 'I think we've said all there is to say,' she insisted tensely, but Enrique shook his head.

'Not nearly,' he responded coolly. 'And I have to tell you that the only reason I am here is because my father is in the hospital in Seville. He had what they call a triple bypass— yes?—ten days ago. Had he not had this operation, he would have received David's letter himself.'

Cassandra was obviously taken aback at this explanation, but although her lips parted she didn't say anything. It was left to David to express his concern and to ask if his grand-father would be home soon. 'We have to go home in less than two weeks,' he explained earnestly. 'Do you think he'll be back before then?'

'It doesn't matter whether he will or not,' declared Cassandra, proving that whatever Enrique had thought she had had nothing to do with the letter. 'I have no intention of allowing you to associate with—with the de Montoyas, David. We've managed without their involvement in our lives for the past nine years. I have no desire to change the status quo.'

'But I have,' cried David indignantly, a sulky curve pulling down the corners of his lips. Lips which were distinctly like his own, noticed Enrique unwillingly. 'They're my family, just as much as you and Grandad are.'

Enrique had never thought he would ever feel sorry for Cassandra, but he did then. Her face, which had been flushed with anger, became almost dangerously pale, and the hand she lifted to push back the heavy weight of her hair was trembling.

'But they don't want you, David,' she said, her voice break-ing under the strain. 'Do you?' She looked at Enrique with eyes he was uneasily aware were filled with tears. 'Do you? Dammit, tell him the truth, can't you?'

*   *   *

It was after eight o'clock before Enrique got back to Tuarega. It hadn't been that late when he'd left Punta del Lobo, but he'd spent at least an hour driving aimlessly along the coastal road, trying to come to terms with what he'd learned.

God! His hands tightened on the wheel of the Mercedes. He couldn't quite believe what had happened. At no time had either he or his father imagined that the woman who had married his brother and who had been widowed less than twenty-four hours later could have conceived a child. And yet she had. There was no doubt that David was a de Montoya.

But she hadn't known a thing about the letter. Her reaction had proved that. As the boy had said, he'd taken it upon himself to write to Julio de Montoya. The letter had been posted before he and his mother had left England.

He groaned.

Of course, it was tempting to shift all the blame onto Cassandra. She should have known what her son had done. He was only nine years old, *por el amor de Dios*. How difficult could it be to keep track of his movements?

But he also knew that he was not speaking from personal experience. And just because the sons and daughters of his close friends were fairly biddable that was no reason to suppose all children were the same. Indeed, he thought wryly, it could be argued that David was already exhibiting facets of his de Montoya heritage.

At the same time he felt a searing sense of injustice that Cassandra had kept the boy's existence from them. And that, without David's intervention, they might never have learned that Antonio had had a son.

Yet could he wholly condemn her for it? After what had happened—after what *he* had tried to do—she probably thought she'd had every right, after Antonio was killed, to cut the de Montoyas out of her life.

But, God, his father was going to get such a shock. If he'd known of the boy's existence, Enrique knew he would have moved heaven and earth to gain custody of the boy. Whatever he'd thought of Cassandra, whatever he'd done to try and stop their marriage, David was his grandson. His only grandson to date. And, where Julio de Montoya was concerned, blood was everything.

Which was probably one of the main reasons why Cassandra had kept the information from them, Enrique acknowledged shrewdly. She knew better than anyone how ruthless his father could be—how ruthless *he* had been in pursuit of his father's wishes.

But he didn't want to think about that now. This was not the time to be feeling the twinges of conscience. He had to remember how Cassandra had seduced Antonio away from his family, his duty, and the girl he had been engaged to marry. She hadn't shown any conscience, any remorse, not even when—

He took a deep breath. No. He would not get into his own role in the affair. The fact that it had ended in tragedy was enough to warrant any sense of outrage he might feel. Cassandra had destroyed so much: Antonio's honour, his loyalty, his future. Was it possible that his brother had found out what a faithless bitch his new wife was and that was why he'd crashed the car as they drove to the south of England on honeymoon?

No! Once again, he couldn't accept that. If he did, it would mean that Antonio had found out what Enrique and his father had tried to do. Surely, in those circumstances, Cassandra would have wanted him to know, would have wanted him to suffer as she was surely suffering now.

His jaw compressed. Thankfully he had succeeded in hiding the extent of the devastation David's appearance had had on him. As far as Cassandra was concerned his shock had been short-lived, swiftly superseded by the anger he'd felt at her deception. No doubt she believed him to be entirely without feeling, and perhaps it was better if it stayed that way. But how the hell was he going to tell his father?

He shook his head. It would have been so much easier ten years ago. Then, Julio de Montoya had been a strong and dominant man, perfectly capable of handling any situation, with a merciless disregard for anyone who got in his way. He had ruled Tuarega with a rod of iron, and that was why he had found it so hard to accept when Antonio had defied him and insisted he wanted to marry the English girl he'd met while he was at college in London. Julio would have done almost anything to stop that marriage, even to the extent of sending his elder son to England with orders to use any means at his disposal to prevent it.

Enrique's nostrils flared with sudden self-derision. That he hadn't succeeded had always been a source of bitterness between himself and his father. He doubted Julio had ever forgiven him entirely for his failure, but his father had never known what had really happened, why Enrique had returned home without achieving his objective.

He could have stopped the wedding. If he'd told Antonio the truth, he was fairly sure his brother would have called it off. But he hadn't said a thing. Because he'd been too ashamed of what he'd done; because he'd had only disgust for his part in it. He'd flown back to Spain knowing that Cassandra had won.

But had she? Now he was not so sure, and he despised himself for his weakness where she was concerned.

It was dark as he drove up through the valley where his family had lived for hundreds of years. Lights glinted from narrow windows in the village and the floodlit spire of San Tomás's church was a reassuring sight. It was easy to believe that nothing changed here, that the ghosts of his ancestors would see and recognise the sights and sounds of other centuries in the immediacy of the twenty-first, but he knew better. There had been many changes, most particularly during General Franco's years as president. But fortunately the political climate in this rural area had never mirrored that found in the cities, and as he accelerated past the fields and paddocks where his *toros bravos*, or fighting bulls, were grazing, he felt a sense of pride in his family's achievements.

But that was short-lived. Thinking of his family reminded him that he had promised to ring his mother this evening. She was staying at the *apartamento* in Seville while her husband was in the hospital there and Enrique had said he would ring no later than seven o'clock. It was long past that time now, and he was ashamed to admit that for the past few hours he had given little thought to his responsibilities.

His mother would be sure to think that he'd forgotten, or that he simply didn't care. Since Julio's illness Elena de Montoya had become over-sensitive, looking for slights where none were intended, as if she was afraid that her husband's incapacity somehow affected her authority. Perhaps she feared that if Julio died Enrique would no longer have respect for her, which was ridiculous.

Still, it was true that since Antonio's death she had come to depend on him more and more. Julio's heart attack some months ago had only increased her demands on his time, and, although Enrique knew it was only to be expected in the circumstances, it wasn't always easy to balance his own needs with those of his parents.

Enrique brought the powerful car to a halt beside the arched colonnade that had once fronted a coach house and which now provided garaging for the estate's many motor vehicles. Years ago, Enrique's grandfather had kept a shining Hispano-Suiza here, and he remembered being allowed to ride in the front of the car on special occasions. He also remembered the punishment he'd received when the old man had found out he had taken the car out alone. He'd been afraid he'd never be allowed to have a car of his own.

But now was not the time to be having memories about the past. He knew it was seeing Cassandra again, meeting the boy, remembering what had happened ten years ago, that was responsible for his reminiscing about happier times. But the past wasn't going to help him now. Somehow he had to decide what he was going to do about the present, and, although he intended to ring his mother, there was no way on earth he could tell her where he had been.

Or what had happened, he conceded, nodding to the man who had emerged from the building to take charge of the car. As he strode across the forecourt to the magnificent entrance of the *palacio* his mind was already busy finding excuses for his tardy behaviour.

Hardly noticing the intricately carved doorway, with its

wrought-iron façade, he strode through a high-ceilinged entry that was distinctly Moorish in design. With a carved ceiling and tiled walls, this was the oldest part of the *palacio* and displayed its heritage in a dozen different ways. Enrique had always believed that Tuarega owed its name to the wild tribe of the Sahara, whose influence had spread beyond the shores of North Africa. But, whatever its history, there was little doubt that it owed its origins to the Saracen invaders who had occupied this part of Spain at the time of the crusades.

Generations of Spanish conquerors had followed them, of course, and much of the present building had been erected in more recent centuries. But the *palacio* had retained its atmosphere of light and coolness and space, successive craftsmen sustaining the delicacy of design that had characterised its Muslim architecture.

The courtyard, where he had eaten breakfast that morning, was immediately ahead of him, but Enrique turned left before reaching the outer doors, mounting a flight of marble stairs to an upper landing. One of the *palacio's* many retainers stopped him to ask if he had eaten, but Enrique wasn't interested in food. First he had to ring his mother, then he had to try and take stock of what his options were. And what he was going to do about them.

Cassandra had given him no latitude. As far as she was concerned he was sure she would prefer to consign him and all his family to hell. She hadn't even let him talk to David, with or without her presence. She'd dragged the boy away into the *pensión*, probably hoping that she never had to see him again.

Which was decidedly naïve, he conceded grimly, thrusting open the door into his apartments and consigning his tie to the nearest surface. Whatever his own feelings in the matter might be, there was no way he could ignore the fact that David was his nephew. His parting words to the boy—that they would meet again, and soon—had been met with a cold 'Over my dead body!' from his mother, but Enrique was not deterred. Whether Cassandra chose to make this easy or not was of no interest to him. David was a de Montoya. Sooner or later he would have to learn what that meant.

CHAPTER THREE

CASSANDRA propped her chin on her hands and stared wearily across the table at her son's sulky face. She ought to be really angry with him, and she was, but she couldn't help feeling the tiniest bit of sympathy, too.

After all, it wasn't his fault that she'd never told him the truth about his de Montoya relations. She'd always avoided any discussion of her late husband's family, hoping, pointlessly as it had turned out, that David would accept the fact that they and his mother just didn't get on. It wasn't as if he was short of an extended family. Cassandra's two sisters were both married with children of their own. David had aunts and uncles and cousins, as well as his maternal grandfather to call on. Foolishly, she had thought that would be enough.

Clearly, it hadn't been. Like his father before him, David was far too intelligent to accept her prevarication. But to go through her things, to seek out Antonio's passport and write secretly to Julio de Montoya without even telling her what he'd done... Well, she didn't know how she was going to forgive him for that.

She sighed, wondering what the chances were of them getting an earlier flight home. Not very good, she surmised, remembering how full the plane had been on the journey out. Besides, she'd paid for a two-week holiday package and if she wanted to change the return date she would obviously have to pay extra for their seats.

Not an option she wanted to consider. She had already spent over her budget in coming here and she was loath to ask her father to bail them out. That, too, would entail more explanations than she was prepared to face at present.

'Are you going to maintain this ridiculous silence for much longer?' she enquired at last, forcing her son to look up from the scrambled eggs and bacon he had ordered in spite of her protests. A fried breakfast was far too heavy in this climate, in her opinion, but David had not been in the mood to compromise. 'Because if you are,' she added, 'I'll leave you to it.'

David emptied his mouth of food, took a gulp of orange juice, and then regarded her with accusing eyes. 'Do I get a choice?' he enquired insolently, and Cassandra knew a totally uncharacteristic desire to smack him.

'I won't be spoken to like this, David,' she said, folding her napkin and placing it beside her plate. She, herself, had eaten nothing, and the sight of the greasy food was enough to turn her stomach. 'I realise you think you have some justification for acting this way, but you've got no idea what a nest of vipers you're uncovering.'

'A nest of vipers,' scoffed her son, around another mouthful of egg. 'You don't know what you're talking about. If you ask me, you're just jealous because Uncle Enrique liked me.'

Jealous!

Cassandra's nails dug into her palms. 'You think so?' she said, the urge to wipe the smug look off his face becoming almost overwhelming. 'And what would you know about it?'

'I know Uncle Enrique is nice, really nice,' declared her son staunchly. 'Gosh, you were so rude to him, Mum! It's a wonder he even wants to see me again.'

Cassandra pressed her lips together, feeling the unwelcome prick of tears behind her eyes. Oh, yes, she wanted to say, Enrique de Montoya wants to see you again. Now that he knows I have a son, he'll do everything he can to take you away from me.

But, of course, she couldn't tell her son that. She couldn't be so cruel. Apart from anything else, it was unlikely he would believe her. In David's world, people were exactly what they appeared to be; they said what they thought. They didn't lie or cheat, or use any means in their power to destroy someone else. Why frighten him unnecessarily? He would learn soon enough that the de Montoyas would do anything to gain their own ends.

'Anyway, I think you should tell him you're sorry when you see him again,' went on David, scraping up the last of his eggs with his fork. He looked up, his dark eyes a haunting reminder of the past. 'We are going to see him again, aren't we, Mum?'

Cassandra hesitated. 'I don't think so. I've decided to cut the holiday short,' she said, even though she hadn't decided any such thing until that moment. 'I'm going to find out whether we can get a flight home later today—'

'No!' David sprang up from his seat in dismay, and the family of holidaymakers at the nearby table turned curious eyes to see what was going on. 'I won't go,' he said, not caring what anyone else thought of his behaviour. 'You can't make me.'

'Sit down, David.'

Cassandra was embarrassed, but her son was beyond being reasoned with. 'I won't sit down,' he declared. 'I want to see Uncle Enrique again. I want to see my grandfather. Why shouldn't I?'

'*Sit down!*'

This time Cassandra got half out of her seat and, as if realising he wasn't doing himself any favours by making it impossible for his mother to face her fellow guests, he subsided unwillingly into his seat.

'Now, listen to me,' said Cassandra, her voice thick with emotion, 'you'll do exactly as I tell you. You're nine years old, David. I have every right to demand that you do as I say.'

David's expression was sulky, but Cassandra was relieved to see that there were tears in his eyes now. 'But why are you being so awful?' he exclaimed huskily. 'You always said you loved my father. Was that just a lie?'

'No!' Cassandra gave an inward groan. 'I did love him. More than you can ever know.'

'Then—'

'But your father wasn't like the rest of his family,' she continued urgently. 'He was—sweet; gentle. He—he was prepared to risk the wrath of his own family just so we could be together.'

David frowned. 'Are you saying they tried to stop you getting married?'

Cassandra's stomach lurched. 'Something like that.'

'So when you said you didn't get on with Dad's family, what you really meant was that they didn't get on with you?'

God, Cassandra really didn't want to talk about this.

'I—suppose so,' she agreed tensely.

'But that doesn't mean they don't want to know you now,' protested David, his eagerness showing in his face. 'Dad died, what? Ten years ago?'

'Nearly.'

'So...' He shrugged. 'They've obviously changed their minds. Why else would Uncle Enrique come here to meet us?'

'Because of *you*,' cried his mother fiercely, realising too late that she had spoken a little too vehemently. 'I mean,' she said, modifying her tone, 'naturally they want to meet you. You're your father's son.'

'And yours,' put in David at once. 'And once they get to know you—'

'They're not going to get to know me,' said Cassandra desperately. 'Haven't you been listening to a word I've said? I never want to see any of the de Montoyas again.'

David's face crumpled. 'You don't mean that.'

'I do mean it.' Cassandra felt dreadful but she had to go on. 'I know you're disappointed, but if we can't get a flight home, I'm going to see if it's possible for us to move to another *pensión* along the coast—'

'No!'

'Yes.' Cassandra was determined. 'I'm prepared to compromise. I know you've been looking forward to this holiday, and I don't want to deprive you of it, so perhaps we can move to another resort.'

'I don't want to move to another resort,' protested David unhappily. 'I like it here. I've made friends here.'

'You'll make friends wherever we go.'

'No, I won't.'

'Of course you will.'

'But—'

'But what?'

David shook his head, apparently deciding he'd argued long enough. 'Nothing,' he muttered, and then looked considerably relieved when Horst Kaufman and his parents stopped at their table.

The German family had been having breakfast on the terrace and now they all smiled down at David and his mother.

'Good morning, Mrs de Montoya,' said Franz Kaufman cheerfully. 'It is another lovely day, yes?'

'Oh—yes.' Cassandra managed a polite smile in return. Then, noticing their more formal clothes, 'Are you going off for the day?'

'Yes. We are going to Ortegar, where we believe there is a leisure facility for the children.' It was Frau Kaufman who answered, and Cassandra couldn't help but admire their grasp of her language. 'A water park and such. We wondered if you would permit David to come with us?'

'Oh.'

Cassandra was nonplussed. She hardly knew the Kaufmans and the idea of allowing David to go off with them for the day was not something she would normally countenance. But, she reminded herself, she was going to spend the day trying to change their hotel arrangements, and going off with Horst and his family might be just what her son needed to put all thoughts of the de Montoyas out of his head.

'Can I, Mum? Can I?'

David was clearly enthusiastic, and, putting her own doubts aside, Cassandra lifted her shoulders in a helpless gesture. 'I—I don't know what to say.'

'We would take great care of him, of course,' put in Franz Kaufman heartily, patting David on the shoulder. 'And as he and Horst get along together so well…'

'We do. We do.'

David gazed at her with wide appealing eyes, and deciding that anything was better than having him dragging after her all day, making his feelings felt, Cassandra sighed.

'Well, all right,' she agreed, earning a whoop from both children. 'Um—where did you say you were going?'

'Ortegar,' said Frau Kaufman at once, and Cassandra frowned.

'Ortegar?' she said. 'Where is that exactly?'

'It is along the coast. Near Cadiz,' answered Franz a little impatiently. 'Maybe twenty miles from here, that is all.'

And probably twenty miles nearer Tuarega, thought Cassandra, moistening her lips. She knew that because she had scanned the map very thoroughly before agreeing to David's choice of destination.

Her heartbeat quickened. David's choice of destination, she realised unsteadily. Goodness, how long had her son been planning to write to his grandfather?

'I'll go and get ready,' said David eagerly, and she wondered if he suspected what she was thinking. 'I won't be long.'

'I'll come with you,' murmured Cassandra, getting up from her chair and giving the Kaufmans another polite smile. 'If you'll excuse me.'

'We will be waiting out front.' Franz Kaufman nodded his approval, and Cassandra was left with the uneasy feeling that she had been out-manoeuvred by her son again.

David had already bundled a towel and his swimming trunks into his backpack by the time she reached their room. He had evidently raced up the stairs and she tried not to wonder if he was desperate to get away.

'Do you need any money?' she asked, picking up a discarded tee shirt from the floor, but David only shook his head and edged towards the door.

'I've got four hundred pesetas. That's enough,' he said quickly, and his mother stared at him.

'That's less than two pounds,' she exclaimed. 'You don't know how much it will cost to get into the leisure park.'

'You can pay Herr Kaufman when we get back,' said David impatiently. 'Come on, Mum. They're waiting for me.'

Not that urgently, thought Cassandra unhappily, but she had given her word. 'All right,' she said, accepting his dutiful peck on her cheek. 'Be good.'

'I will.' David headed out of the door with a triumphant grin on his face. 'See you later.'

*   *   *

Sanchia's red sports car was just pulling up outside the *palacio* when Enrique came out of the building. Sanchia herself, tall and dark and exotically beautiful, emerged from the vehicle, smoothing down the narrow skirt of the green linen suit that barely skimmed her knees.

Once his brother's fiancé, Sanchia had swiftly recovered from that fiasco. Within a year, she had married a distant relative of the Spanish royal family, and when her elderly husband died leaving her a wealthy widow, she had immediately transferred her affections to her late fiancé's brother, making Enrique wonder if that hadn't been her objective all along.

But perhaps he was being conceited, he thought now. Sanchia had been heartbroken when Antonio had married an Englishwoman and had then been killed almost before the ink on the marriage licence was dry. She had turned to him then, but he hadn't imagined that her plea for his affection had been anything more than a natural response to the circumstances she'd found herself in. After all, Sanchia's family had never had a lot of money and it must have been quite a blow when her wealthy fiancé abandoned her less than three months before their wedding.

In any event, Enrique had made it quite plain then that he was not interested in taking up where his brother had left off. He liked Sanchia well enough, he always had, but the idea of taking her to bed because his brother had let her down was anathema to him. He had been grieving, too, and not just because his brother was dead. He had let Antonio down, and he'd found it hard to live with himself at that time.

Now, things were different. Sanchia had been married and widowed, and he himself was that much older and more willing to accept that life could all too easily deal you a rotten hand. The relationship he had with Sanchia these days suited both of them. He doubted he would ever get married, despite what his father had had to say about it, and, although Sanchia might hope that he'd change his mind, she was not, and never could be, the only woman in his life.

Which was probably why he felt such an unexpected surge

of impatience at her appearance this morning. His thoughts were focused on what he planned to do today and Sanchia could play no part in that.

She, of course, knew nothing of the events of yesterday. Even though there'd been a message from her waiting on his answering machine when he'd got back last night, he hadn't returned her call, which probably explained her arrival now.

'Querido!' she exclaimed, her use of the Spanish word for 'darling' sounding warm and intimate on her tongue. She reached up to kiss him, pouting when her lips only brushed his cheek, before surveying his casual appearance with some disappointment. 'You are going out? I was hoping we might spend the day together.'

'I am sorry.' Enrique was aware that his navy tee shirt and cargo trousers were not his usual attire, but they were less likely to attract attention in a holiday resort than the three-piece suit he'd worn the day before. 'I have got—some business to attend to.'

'Dressed like this?' Sanchia twined her fingers into the leather cord that he'd tied at his waist. 'I cannot see you visiting one of your clients in a tee shirt.'

'Did I say I was going to visit one of my clients?' asked Enrique rather more curtly than he had intended. He disentangled her fingers from the cord and stepped back from her. 'It is a personal matter,' he appended, feeling obliged to give her some sort of explanation. 'Really. I have got to go.'

'Is it another woman?' she demanded, and just for a moment he felt a surge of resentment that she should feel she had the right to question his actions.

But then common sense reasserted itself. Why shouldn't she feel she had some rights where he was concerned? They had been seeing one another for months, after all.

'Not in the way you mean,' he assured her, his thin smile hardly a reassurance. Then, belatedly, 'Perhaps I can ring you later?'

Sanchia's lips tightened. 'You are not going to tell me where you are going?'

'No.' There was no ambivalence on that score.

Her mouth trembled now. 'Enrique...'

His irritation was totally unwarranted, and he despised himself for it. But, dammit, he wanted to get to Punta del Lobo before Cassandra had time to disappear again. 'Look,' he said reasonably, 'this does not concern you—us. It is—something to do with my father. A confidential matter I have to attend to.'

Sanchia's jaw dropped. 'Your father has been having an affair?'

'No!' Enrique was horrified that she should even think such a thing.

'But you said it did involve another woman,' she reminded him, and Enrique wished he'd kept his mouth shut.

'I also said, not in the way you mean,' he declared shortly. 'It is just—' *Dios*, what could he say? '—an unexpected complication.'

'That involves a woman?'

'Only indirectly.'

That, at least, was true, although Enrique could feel his stomach tighten as he thought of confronting Cassandra again. *Dios*, he hated that woman, he thought savagely. If only he could tell Sanchia how he really felt, she would have no further cause for concern.

'*Muy bien.*' She pivoted on her high heels and, waiting for him to fall into step beside her, she started towards her car. 'But you will ring me later this morning, *sí*?'

'Make it this afternoon,' said Enrique, suppressing a sigh. 'If I cannot reach you at home, I will call your mobile.'

'Which will not be switched off as yours was last night,' remarked Sanchia waspishly, inspiring another twinge of irritation. Dammit, when had they got to the point where every move he made had to be justified?

'I will ring,' he assured her, making no promises of when that would be. He swung open the door of the scarlet convertible. '*Adiós!*'

CHAPTER FOUR

CASSANDRA trudged back to the lodging house with a heavy heart. She had wasted the whole morning waiting to see her holiday representative to try and get David and herself transferred to an alternative *pensión*, but she was no further forward.

The trouble was, the kind of accommodation she and her son could afford was in short supply and, without paying a huge supplement and moving to a hotel, they were stuck. The young rep who was based at the nearby Hotel Miramar had been very polite, but after spending the morning dealing with other holidaymakers' complaints, she was naturally puzzled by Cassandra's request. Particularly as the only excuse she could offer for wanting to leave the Pensión del Mar was because Punta del Lobo was too quiet. The girl had probably thought she was used to frequenting bars and nightclubs, thought Cassandra unhappily. And what kind of a mother did that make her appear to be?

It was all Enrique de Montoya's fault, she thought resentfully. If he hadn't turned up and ruined what had promised to be the first really good holiday they had had in ages, she wouldn't have had to tell lies to anyone, or now have to face the prospect of David's disappointment when he discovered their options had narrowed. As far as she could see, she only had one alternative: to bring the date for their homeward journey forward. Whatever it cost.

And, as she approached the *pensión*, she was forced to admit that it wasn't just the de Montoyas' fault that she was in this position. David had to take his share of the blame. All right, perhaps she should have been more honest with him right from the beginning, but surely he had known that what

37

he was doing was wrong? Wasn't that why he had kept the letter a secret from her?

She turned in at the gate of the *pensión*, tipping her head back to ease the tension in her neck, and then felt a quivering start in the pit of her stomach. As she looked ahead again, she saw a man rising from the low wall that bordered the terrace, where chairs and tables offered an alternative to eating indoors. The striped canopy, which gave the Pensión del Mar its individuality, formed a protective shade from the rays of the midday sun, but it also cast a shadow that Cassandra at first thought had deceived her eyes. But, no, she was not mistaken. It was Enrique who had been sitting there, waiting for her, like the predator she knew him to be.

But, as always, he looked cool and composed, his lean muscled frame emphasised by a tight-fitting navy tee shirt and loose cotton trousers. Despite herself, she felt her senses stir at his dark, powerful masculinity, and it was that much harder to steel herself against him.

'What are you doing here?' she asked, taking the offensive before he could disconcert her, and he gave her a retiring look.

'Where is he?' he demanded, looking beyond her, and she was inordinately grateful that the Kaufmans had taken David out for the day.

'He's not here,' she said, deciding to let him make what he liked of that. 'You've wasted your time in coming here.'

Enrique's eyes grew colder, if that were at all possible. He was already regarding her with icy contempt, and she was unhappily aware that again he had found her looking hot and dishevelled. But after a morning sitting in the open foyer of the Miramar, which was not air-conditioned and where she had not been offered any refreshment, she was damp and sweaty. Her hair, which she should really have had cut before she came away, was clinging to the nape of her neck, and her cropped sleeveless top and cotton shorts fairly shrieked of their chainstore origins.

But what did it matter what he thought of her? she asked herself impatiently. However she looked, he was not going to alter his opinion of her or of David, and, even if she'd been voted the world's greatest mum, the de Montoyas would still be looking for a way to take David away from her.

'Where is he?' Enrique asked again, and this time she decided not to prevaricate.

'He's gone out with friends,' she replied, making an abortive little foray to go past him, but he stepped into her path.

'What friends?' His dark eyes bored into her. 'The Kaufmans?'

'Got it in one,' said Cassandra, acknowledging that Enrique never forgot a name. 'Now, if you'll excuse me...'

Enrique said something that sounded suspiciously like an oath before his hard fingers fastened about her forearm. 'Do not be silly, Cassandra,' he intoned wearily. 'You are not going anywhere and you know it.'

She didn't attempt to shake him off. It wouldn't have done any good and she knew it. But perhaps she could get rid of him in other ways and she widened her eyes challengingly at him as she opened her mouth.

But the scream she'd been about to utter stuck in her throat when he hustled her across the gravelled forecourt of the *pensión*, his words harsh against her ear. 'Make a scene and I may just have to report Señor Movida to the licensing authorities.'

Cassandra stared at him. 'You can't do that. Señor Movida hasn't done anything wrong.'

'I am sure my lawyers could come up with something, if I paid them enough,' retorted Enrique unfeelingly, propelling her around the corner from the *pensión* to where his Mercedes was parked. 'And you, I am equally sure, would not risk that.'

Cassandra trembled. 'You're a bastard, Enrique!'

'Better a bastard than a liar, Cassandra,' he informed her coldly, flicking the switch that unlocked the car. 'Please get in.'

'And if I don't?'

Enrique regarded her with unblinking eyes. 'Do not go there, Cassandra. You are only wasting your time and mine. We need to talk, and you will have to forgive my sensibilities when I say I prefer not to—how is it you say it?—wash my linen in public?'

'Dirty linen,' muttered Cassandra, before she could stop herself, and Enrique's mouth curved into a thin smile.

'Your words, not mine,' he commented, swinging open the nearside door and waiting patiently for her to get into the car. And, when she'd done so with ill grace, unhappily conscious of her bare knees and sun-reddened thighs, he walked round the back of the vehicle and coiled his long length behind the steering wheel. Then, with a derisive glance in her direction, 'Do not look so apprehensive, Cassandra. I do not bite.'

'Don't you?'

Now she held his gaze with hot accusing eyes and then experienced a pang of anguish when he looked away. Was he remembering what she was remembering? she wondered, despising herself for the unwelcome emotions he could still arouse inside her. God, the only memories she should have were bitter ones.

His starting the engine caught her unawares. 'What do you think you're doing?' she cried, diverted from her thoughts, and he lifted his shoulders in a resigned gesture.

'What does it look like I am doing?' he enquired, glancing in the rearview mirror, checking for traffic. 'You didn't think we were going to sit here and talk?'

'Why not?'

'Humour me,' he said tersely, and although Cassandra was fairly sure that nothing she said or did would change his mind, she bit down on her protests. Why should she object when he was leaving the *pensión*? She might even be able to persuade him not to come back.

Or not.

'I'm not going to Tuarega with you,' she blurted suddenly, and Enrique gave a short mirthless laugh as he pulled out of the parking bay.

'I have not invited you to do so,' he observed drily, and she felt the flush of embarrassment deepen the colour in her cheeks. 'I suggest we find a bar where it is unlikely that either of us will meet anyone we know.'

'Don't you mean anyone *you* know?' she snorted, and he gave her a considering look.

'Does it matter?'

'Not to me,' she assured him coldly. 'I just want to get this over with.'

Enrique shook his head. 'We both know that is not going to happen,' he replied flatly. 'You should not have written to my father if you wished to keep your selfish little secret.'

'I didn't write to your father,' Cassandra reminded him fiercely. 'I wouldn't do such a thing.'

'No.' He conceded the point. 'I believe that now.'

'Now?' Cassandra was appalled. 'Do you mean you had any doubts?'

Enrique shrugged. 'I had my reasons.'

'What reasons?' Cassandra stared at him, and then comprehension dawned. 'My God, you did think I'd written the letter, didn't you? You honestly thought I'd want anything from *you*! Or your father!'

Enrique didn't answer her and she was left with the shattering discovery that his opinion of her hadn't changed one bit. He still thought she was a greedy little gold-digger, who had only latched onto his brother because she'd known what his background was.

Pain, like a knife, sliced through her, and she reached unthinkingly for the handle of the door. In that moment she didn't consider that they had left the small town of Punta del Lobo behind, that the car was in traffic and that they were moving at approximately sixty kilometres an hour. Her only need was to get as far away from him as possible as quickly as possible, and even the sudden draught of air that her action elicited only made her feel even more giddy and confused.

She didn't know what might have happened if Enrique hadn't reacted as he had. At that moment she didn't care. But, with a muffled oath, he did two things almost simultaneously: his hand shot out and grasped her arm, anchoring her to her seat, and he swung the big car off the winding coast road, bringing it to a shuddering stop on a sand-strewn verge above towering cliffs.

'*Estas loco?* Are you mad?' he demanded, and she realised it was a measure of the shock he'd had that he'd used his own language and not hers. Then, when she turned a white tear-stained face in his direction, his eyes grew dark and tortured. 'Crazy woman,' he muttered, his voice thick and unfamiliar, and, switching off the engine, he flung himself out of the car.

He went to stand at the edge of the cliffs, the warm wind that blew up from the ocean flattening the loose-fitting trousers against his strong legs. He didn't look back at her, he simply stood there, gazing out at the water, raking long fingers through his hair before bringing them to rest at the back of his neck.

Perhaps he was giving her time to regain her composure, Cassandra pondered uneasily, as sanity reasserted itself. But she didn't think so. Just for a moment there she had glimpsed the real Enrique de Montoya, the passionate man whose feelings couldn't be so coldly contained beneath a mask of studied politeness, and she suspected he had been as shocked as she was.

Nevertheless, however she felt about him, there was little doubt that he had saved her from serious injury or worse. He'd risked his own life by swerving so recklessly off the highway, taking the car within inches of certain disaster, just to prevent her from doing something which, as he'd said, would have been crazy.

What had she been thinking? She trembled as the full extent of her own stupidity swept over her. What good would it have done to throw herself from the car? What would it have achieved? If she'd been killed—God, the very thought of it set her shaking again—who would have looked after David then? Whose claim on her son would have carried the most weight? She didn't need to be a psychic to know that in those circumstances her own family would have been fighting a losing battle.

So why hadn't Enrique let her do it? Or was that what he was doing now? Reproving himself for allowing a God-given opportunity to slip through his fingers? No. However naïve it might make her, she didn't think that either.

She took a breath and then, pushing open her door, she got out of the car. She steadied herself for a moment, with her hand on the top of her door. Then, closing it again, she walked somewhat unsteadily across to where he was standing. The wind buffeted her, too, sending the tumbled mass of her hair about her face, but she only held it back, her eyes on Enrique's taut profile.

'I'm—sorry,' she said after a moment, but although she knew he'd heard her, he didn't look her way.

'Go back to the car.' The words were flat and expressionless. 'I will join you in a moment.'

Cassandra caught her lower lip between her teeth. 'You're right,' she said, forced to go on. 'What I did was crazy! I could have killed us both.'

Now Enrique did look at her, but she gained no reassurance from his blank expression. 'Forget it,' he told her. 'I have.'

Cassandra quivered. 'As you forget everything that doesn't agree with you?' she asked tremulously. 'And everyone?'

Enrique's features contorted. 'I have forgotten nothing,' he assured her harshly, and she shrank from his sudden antagonism.

'Then how do you live with yourself?' she was stung to reply, and with a muffled epithet he brushed past her.

'God knows,' he muttered in his own language, but she understood him. He headed for the car. 'Are you coming?'

The bar he took her to was in the next village. A whitewashed building on the road, it was open at the back, spilling its customers out onto a wood-framed deck above a pebbled beach. Further along, a black jetty jutted out into the blue water, and several small fishing smacks and rowing boats were drawn up onto a strip of sand. Old men sat mending their nets, and, judging by the clientele in the bar, this was not a venue for tourists.

Contrary to what Enrique had said earlier, the bartender knew exactly who he was, and it was obvious from the man's manner that he welcomed his customer. Cassandra guessed, nonetheless, that he was curious about who she was and why Enrique should choose to bring her here, but he knew better than to ask questions. Instead, he escorted them personally to a table on the deck that was shaded by a canvas canopy, and enquired politely what he could get them to drink.

'Wine?' suggested Enrique, looking at Cassandra, and at her indifferent nod he ordered two glasses of Rioja. 'It is served from a barrel here,' he explained as the man walked away, and Cassandra guessed he was only behaving courteously for the other man's benefit.

'What is this place?' she asked, taking her cue from him, and Enrique glanced towards the jetty before looking at her.

'San Augustin,' he said in the same civil tone. 'I used to come here a lot when I was younger. While I was a student, I worked behind the bar for a while until my father found out.'

'And stopped you?' suggested Cassandra unthinkingly, and he nodded.

'My father said a de Montoya should not—well, it is not important what he said,' he appended shortly. 'It is many years now.'

'Yet the bartender remembers you.'

'I did not mean it is so many years since I was here,' he explained. 'José and I, we know one another quite well.'

Cassandra began to smile and then pulled her lips into a straight line again. She was starting to relax with him and that was not good. She had no doubt it would suit him very well, but she had to remember why he had brought her here and it wasn't to exchange anecdotes about the past. Well, not that past anyway, she amended, with a sudden spurt of hysteria.

The bartender returned with their wine and a large plate of what she realised were *tapas*. But not the mass-produced *tapas* that were available in the bars in Punta del Lobo. Something told her that this was the real thing, the fat juicy olives, spiced with herbs, the batter-dipped prawns, the bite-sized pieces of crisply fried fish bearing little resemblance to what she'd seen so far. They smelled wholesome, too, and in other circumstances the cheese that was oozing out of the paper-thin rolls of ham would have made her mouth water.

'Is good, *señor*?' the man enquired, obviously having heard them speaking in English, and Enrique inclined his head.

'*Muy bien, José,*' he responded in his own language. Very good. '*Gracias.*'

The bartender smiled and went away, and Enrique indicated the food. 'Are you hungry?'

'Hardly,' said Cassandra, reluctantly taking a sip of her wine. She hoped it wasn't too intoxicating. She'd had nothing to eat that day and her stomach was already bubbling with apprehension. 'Why did you want to speak to me?'

Enrique hesitated. She noticed he wasn't interested in the food either and, like her, he seemed quite content to concentrate on his wine. His hands, brown and long-fingered, played with the stem of his glass, and she was mesmerised by their sensitive caress. It reminded her far too acutely of how those fingers had felt gripping her wrist, grasping her arm, stroking her naked flesh...

She took a laboured breath as somewhere nearby a guitar began to play. Its music, poignant at times, at others vibrantly sensual, tugged at her emotions, fanning the flames of memories she desperately wanted to forget. She should not have come here, she thought unsteadily. She was still far too vulnerable where he was concerned.

'I think you know why we have to talk,' Enrique said at last, his eyes intent. 'David is a de Montoya. You had no right to keep that from us.'

Cassandra pursed her lips. 'You're sure of that, are you?'

'What? That he is Antonio's son? Of course.'

'What makes you so certain?'

Enrique lay back in his chair, giving her a sardonic look. 'Cassandra, do not play games with me. We both know that he is the image of his father at that age.'

'Is he?'

'Do you wish me to produce a photograph as proof? No, I did not think so. The boy shows his Spanish blood in every way. His eyes, his colouring, his mannerisms. His honesty.'

Cassandra stiffened. 'His honesty?' she demanded caustically. 'Oh, right. You'd know a lot about that.'

A muscle in Enrique's jaw jerked angrily. 'Do not bait me,

Cassandra. What is it they say about glass houses? It is not wise to throw stones, no?'

Cassandra rested her elbows on the table, hunching her shoulders and curling her fingers behind her ears. It would be so easy to burst his bubble, she mused, so easy to explode the myth that David was Antonio's son, but it was seldom wise to give in to temptation, as she knew only too well. Much better to wait to allow the situation to develop, to keep that particular revelation up her sleeve. She had reason to believe that she might need it.

'All right,' she said, allowing him to make what he liked of that, 'perhaps I should have informed your father when David was born. But I had every reason to believe that he— that all of you—wanted nothing more to do with me.'

Enrique's nostrils flared. 'So you decided to take your revenge by keeping the boy's existence a secret from us?'

'It wasn't revenge,' exclaimed Cassandra fiercely, her voice rising. And then, aware that she was attracting the attention of other patrons in the bar, she lowered her tone. 'I mean it. I—I wanted nothing more to do with the de Montoyas.'

'Even though my father was Antonio's father, too? That he is David's grandfather? That David is his only grandson?'

'I didn't know that, did I?' muttered Cassandra, taking a reckless gulp of her wine and almost choking herself. She coughed painfully and her eyes watered and it was several minutes before she could continue. 'I assumed that you'd have married and had children of your own,' she got out at last.

'Did you really?' He was sceptical.

'If I ever thought about it,' she declared defensively. 'I— have to admit, it's not something that's given me sleepless nights.'

Which wasn't entirely true, but Enrique didn't need to know that.

'No,' he said now, his lips twisting. 'Why should you waste your time on something that meant so little to you?'

Cassandra arched brows that were several shades darker than her hair. 'Do you blame me?'

Enrique shrugged, and with sudden urgency she added, 'I've always wondered, what did you tell Antonio?'

Enrique shook his head. 'Why should I tell you? He obviously did not believe me.'

'No.' She looked doubtful. 'He never said anything about it to me.'

'Why would he?' Enrique was harsh. 'My brother, too, was an honourable man.'

'Too?' she mocked him. 'I hope you're not including yourself in that statement.'

'I meant my father,' he retorted coldly. 'And my nephew David, at least understands that family means something.'

'David has a family.' Cassandra quivered in remembrance of why they were here. 'An English family. Who love him.'

'He also has a Spanish family who would love him just as much,' replied Enrique inflexibly. 'Oh, this is getting us nowhere.' He raised his hand and summoned the bartender, but although Cassandra knew a moment's panic that he had decided not to continue their conversation, he merely ordered two more glasses of wine.

The bartender, who brought his order, looked a little dismayed to see that they hadn't touched the *tapas*, but he held his tongue. Cassandra guessed he had taken one look at Enrique's dark face and decided now was not the time to make comments. Instead, he sauntered away with a decidedly defiant swagger.

'Now,' said Enrique, when they were alone again, 'I suggest we try to find some common ground here.' He took a breath. 'We are agreed, are we not, that David is Antonio's son, yes?' And, getting no argument from Cassandra, he continued, 'Very well. It is therefore a question of deciding how and when I am going to break this news to my father.'

Cassandra's throat closed up. 'And then what?' She had the sensation of things moving too fast for her here, of them getting out of control. And she wasn't altogether sure what she could do to stop them. 'We have to go back to England in a couple of days.'

'No.' Enrique was very definite about that. 'You will not

be going back to England until this affair is settled. And, just to put the matter straight, I have to tell you that before you and the boy appeared yesterday I spoke with Señor Movida at the *pensión*. He was kind enough to tell me that your booking is for two weeks. Do we understand one another?'

Cassandra's mouth quivered. 'You think you've got it all worked out, don't you?' She rubbed the end of her nose with a trembling finger. 'You can't tell me what to do.'

'Oh, Cassandra.' Now he sounded weary. 'You must have known how it would be. David wants to know his family— *all* his family. Do you honestly think you have the right to deny him that?'

Cassandra didn't know what to think any more. Her attempt to get away from Punta del Lobo, to return to England without Enrique's knowledge, seemed pointless now. The de Montoyas knew of David's existence. A few hundred miles would not prove any obstacle if they wanted to see him. Besides, it was David's life, David's decision. His letter had proved that. So did she have the right to prevent him from meeting his grandfather if that was what he wanted?

'Will you take me back to the *pensión*?' she asked tightly, her doubts weighing heavily on her conscience. 'David will be back soon.'

'And what will you tell him?'

Cassandra gave him a bitter look. 'Anything but the truth,' she said coldly. 'Can we go?'

CHAPTER FIVE

PUNTA DEL LOBO was quiet in the early-afternoon heat. Most of the shops and boutiques observed the hours of *siesta*, opening again around five o'clock and staying open until late in the evening.

It looked so normal, but Cassandra knew the kind of dislocation that came from feeling one thing and experiencing another. The narrow streets of whitewashed buildings might look familiar, but inside she sensed that nothing was ever going to be normal again.

She was relieved to see that the Kaufmans' hired Fiat was back in its parking space, although she was not looking forward to explaining to David why she had been consorting with a man she had hitherto treated as the enemy. He was bound to wonder why she hadn't told him that Enrique was coming, and even though she could deny having any knowledge of the Spaniard's movements, she suspected David might not believe her.

And, to a degree, he'd have a point. Hadn't she secretly suspected that Enrique might turn up today? Wasn't that why she'd been eager to get away from the *pensión* herself that morning? Only it hadn't worked, she thought dully. She'd forgotten how persistent—how patient—Enrique could be.

The Kaufmans were gathered on the forecourt before the *pensión* and Cassandra expelled a heavy sigh. Although she was glad that they were back, she would have preferred not to have advertised that fact to Enrique. He wouldn't have known the Fiat was their car, and without their physical presence to alert him he might have been inclined to leave.

Yeah, right.

She blew out a breath. She was being naïve. Enrique had

49

come here to see David and he was hardly likely to go away again without achieving his objective.

This time, Enrique parked the Mercedes at the gate and Cassandra pushed open her door with a heavy heart. There was no sign of her son, but she guessed he'd gone into the *pensión* to find her. Summoning a smile for the Kaufmans' benefit, she walked slowly up the path, aware that Enrique was right behind her.

The Kaufmans didn't smile, however, and Cassandra felt the first twinges of anxiety prick at her senses. What was wrong? What had happened? Why were they looking so worried? Oh, God, was David all right?

'You're back early,' she said, stifling her fears beneath a mask of politeness. 'I'm sorry I wasn't here when—'

'Mrs de Montoya! *Señora!*' Franz Kaufman stepped forward then, his plump face flushed with unbecoming colour. 'I am afraid I have some very—disturbing—news.'

'David?' began Cassandra, panic-stricken. 'Something's happened to David—?'

'*Calma, pequeña!*' Once again, Enrique lapsed into his own language to reassure her. Then, looking at Herr Kaufman, he arched an imperious brow. '*Donde esta el chico?*'

Franz Kaufman looked nonplussed. '*Er—no hablo español, señor,*' he said apologetically, and Cassandra could almost taste Enrique's frustration.

'The boy,' he said, his accent suddenly very pronounced. 'David: where is he?'

Franz Kaufman looked from one to the other of them in some alarm. 'I do not know,' he said unhappily, and Cassandra was hardly aware that she had clutched Enrique's arm in her panic. 'He—he has disappeared.'

'Disappeared?' cried Cassandra, her face draining of all colour. 'What do you mean, disappeared? Where did he disappear? Have you lost him?'

'Cassandra…' Enrique's voice was more reassuring than she would have thought possible. 'Let Herr Kaufman explain what has happened. We will not achieve anything by making as yet unfounded accusations, no?'

'I am so sorry, *señora*.' Franz Kaufman addressed his remarks to Cassandra now, and she saw how both Frau Kaufman and Horst moved closer to him as he spoke, as if seeking his protection. 'We went, as you know, to the water park at Ortegar, and both the boys wanted to go swimming in the wave pool.'

'And?'

Now Enrique was getting impatient, and the German hurried on with his explanation. 'There were lots of children in the pool, and the last we saw of David—'

'The last?' whispered Cassandra faintly, her nails digging unconsciously into Enrique's arm, and he turned to give her a sympathetic look.

'He seemed so content,' continued Franz Kaufman helplessly, putting an unknowing possessive hand on his son's shoulder. 'Frau Kaufman and I, we felt quite able to leave the boys to play while we went to the cafeteria to have a coffee.'

'You left them?' exclaimed Cassandra, but once again Enrique gave her a warning stare.

'It was not our fault,' put in Frau Kaufman suddenly, apparently deciding her husband was being too conciliatory. 'Horst said that David told him he was going down the—what is it they call it, Franz? The chute, *ja*? Horst did not want to go with him.' She shrugged. 'David did not come back.'

'Oh, God!'

Cassandra felt sick. She had thought that things couldn't get worse, but they had. David could be anywhere, with anyone. Dear God, she had heard such stories about boys of his age being lured away by unscrupulous men. Right this minute, he could be fighting for his life—

She caught her breath. He might even now be lying at the bottom of the chute in the water park. She hadn't thought of that. Oh, God! What was she going to do?

A sob escaped her, and Enrique, who had been asking more questions of the other family, turned to her with sudden concern.

'*Querida*,' he said softly, using an endearment she had never thought to hear from him again. 'Cassandra, try and be positive. It may be that David lost his way back to the wave pool. Ortegar is a big complex. He could be with the director right now, waiting for someone to come and collect him.'

'Do you think so?' Cassandra realised belatedly that she was still gripping Enrique's arm and immediately dropped her hands to her sides. She shook her head. 'I've got to go there.' She hesitated, and then added in a low voice, 'Will you take me?'

'I would be happy to take you, *señora*,' declared Herr Kaufman before Enrique could respond. He ignored his wife's disapproving glare and touched Cassandra's arm. 'It is the least I can do.'

'Oh, well—'

Cassandra was turning to him when Enrique spoke. 'That will not be necessary, *señor*,' he said firmly. 'David is my nephew. Naturally, I am the one to escort Señora de Montoya to Ortegar.'

'If you say so.' Herr Kaufman's manner was stiff now, as if Enrique's command of the situation had devalued his offer and he was offended by it. 'But I must say, we searched the complex very thoroughly, and there was no sign of your son, *señora*.'

Cassandra shook her head, unable to answer him. Didn't he realise that that was the last thing she wanted to hear? If David had disappeared, couldn't he allow her to hope for just a little while longer?

'That was why we came back here,' added his wife shortly. 'We cut our day short because we hoped that if David had got lost, he might have got a lift back.'

'A lift?' Cassandra's throat was dry. 'Who with?'

'There were plenty of English people there,' said Frau Kaufman defensively. 'He could have gone with any one of them.'

'But David's not like that,' protested Cassandra, and then, catching Enrique's eyes on her, she shut up. He was right. There was no point in attributing blame. She should know, better than anyone, that David wasn't always predictable.

The sound of a mobile phone ringing cut into their

exchange. It was close, but not that close, and she was hardly surprised when Enrique excused himself and headed for the Mercedes.

She watched him anxiously. There was no reason for her to feel apprehensive about that phone call, but she did. Yet that was stupid. No one knew that Enrique was with her. Certainly no one at the Ortegar water park.

Enrique picked up the small phone and flicked open the mouthpiece. '*Sí?*' she heard him say, with obvious impatience, and then whatever was being relayed to him from the other end of the connection caused his expression to darken in obvious disbelief.

Cassandra took an involuntary step towards him. Somehow, she didn't know how, she sensed that the call had to do with David, and she was suddenly reminded of her doubts earlier in the day. Doubts about David going to Ortegar, about Ortegar's closer proximity to the de Montoya estate...

Pressing a hand to her throat, she continued down the path, and Enrique watched her approach with dark, enigmatic eyes. *Please,* she prayed silently, *let David be all right.*

Enrique finished the call almost simultaneously with her reaching the car, and tossed the phone back onto the console. 'He is at Tuarega,' he said shortly, and she didn't know whether he was relieved or angry. He went past her to tell the Kaufmans, and Cassandra crumpled against the wing. A momentary dizziness assailed her. He was safe! David was safe! Thank God!

It was only when Enrique came striding back to the Mercedes that she felt the beginnings of her own anger towards her son. No wonder he had been so eager to go out with the Kaufmans, she thought bitterly. He must have known exactly what he was going to do. Only Enrique had thwarted him by coming here.

'Get in,' said Enrique, swinging open the door, and Cassandra looked up at him with wary eyes.

'Aren't you going to tell me how he got to Tuarega?' she asked, aware that it was difficult to keep the tremor out of her voice. But she felt so helpless, so angry with her son. She couldn't believe he had been so reckless.

'I will tell you on the way,' Enrique said tersely. 'Come: we are wasting time.'

Cassandra hesitated, but then, glancing back at the other family, who were still clustered together outside the *pensión*, she decided to do as he said. She didn't want to get into explanations with the Kaufmans, explanations she couldn't begin to justify. Time enough for that later, when she'd had the opportunity to gather her thoughts.

'I ought to get changed,' she murmured, reluctant to appear before any members of his family in her cropped tee shirt and shorts, but Enrique merely gave her a considering look.

'I thought you were worried about your son,' he remarked, and the gentleness that had been in his voice earlier had all disappeared now.

Cassandra frowned. 'I am.'

'Get in, then,' he directed, walking round the bonnet to get behind the wheel. 'It is an hour's drive to Tuarega. Better not to give him time to have second thoughts, no?'

Cassandra scrambled into her seat without further ado. 'Do you think that's likely?' she asked, unable to prevent the question, and Enrique grimaced.

'No,' he said, starting the engine. 'I think he is exactly where he intended to be all along. Unfortunately, there was no one but my steward around to welcome him.'

'Your steward?' Cassandra glanced sideways at him as the car pulled away from the *pensión*. 'Was that who rang?'

Enrique nodded. 'It was.'

'Your mother's away?'

'My mother is staying at the *apartamento* in Seville,' he replied. 'So that she can be near my father.' His lips twisted with sudden irony. *'Gracias a Dios!'*

Cassandra stiffened. 'You've changed your mind about telling your parents about David?' she asked swiftly, but his reaction mocked her fleeting optimism.

'You wish,' he retorted with a short unfeeling laugh, and her eyes dropped to her hands, twisted together in her lap.

What had she expected? she chided herself. Enrique's only concern was the shock it would give the older de Montoyas to learn that they had a grandson after all these years. He didn't care about her feelings. He never had. She had only to remember the way he'd ignored her at his brother's funeral to know that Enrique believed she deserved nothing but his contempt.

Her eyes filled with tears, blocking her nose and making it difficult for her to breathe. She turned her head away so that he wouldn't notice and stared out at the beauty of the scenery surrounding them.

They had left Punta del Lobo behind and the busy coastal area was giving way to bare plains and fertile valleys. *Cortijos*, or farms, where white-painted cottages hid amongst avenues of citrus fruits and olive trees, followed the contours of hills that were tinged with purple in the lengthening shadows of late afternoon.

This had been her husband's homeland, she reminded herself, rubbing an impatient finger along the ridge of her nose. He had been familiar with these hills, these valleys, and, because the blood of the de Montoyas ran in David's veins, wasn't it natural that he should feel some affinity with it, too?

She looked down at her hands again, only this time her eyes were drawn to Enrique's feet in their expensive leather loafers. He wasn't wearing any socks, she noticed, his narrow ankles disappearing beneath the uncuffed hems of his cotton trousers. They were loose-fitting around his calves, only defining the body beneath when they reached his knees and the powerful thighs above them. His tee shirt was tucked into the drawstring waistband, and the leather cords hung down between his legs, drawing her attention to the unmistakable bulge of his sex…

God!

She dragged her eyes away from his crotch, feeling a film of sweat breaking out on her upper lip. This was crazy! *Crazy!* How could she be thinking such thoughts about a man who had done his best to ruin her life? She must be out of her mind.

'I suppose you think it is all my fault?'

His words broke into the turmoil of her thoughts, and for a moment she could only gaze at him, uncomprehending. 'I beg your—?'

'For David's running away from the Kaufmans,' prompted Enrique, his brows drawing together when he saw her flushed cheeks and glittering eyes. 'What is it? What is wrong? Are you ill?'

Only stressed out, she wanted to say bitterly, but she could hardly blame him for the shameful direction of her thoughts. That was all her doing, and she despised herself for allowing sex to colour her reactions to him.

'Just—hot,' she said instead, raising her hands to lift the weight of her hair away from her neck. Despite the car's air-conditioning system, her body seemed to be on some other planet. And it was only when she realised how the action caused her breasts to press provocatively against the thin fabric of her top that she quickly lowered her arms again. She wiped a knuckle surreptitiously over her upper lip. 'Um—is it much further?'

'Perhaps—twenty minutes,' answered Enrique tightly, and she guessed he'd noticed her embarrassment. Or perhaps she'd embarrassed him, she considered wryly. Though it wasn't likely. Enrique de Montoya was always in control of himself and his actions.

She was easing her thighs off the seat, allowing some air to pass between her skin and the leather, when he glanced her way again. 'You are not comfortable?'

'I'm fine,' she lied hurriedly. Then, forcing herself to look about her, 'Herr Kaufman said that your father's estate is famous for the bulls it breeds.' She took a steadying breath. 'I didn't know he was a farmer.'

'A farmer?' Enrique spoke drily. 'Is that what Kaufman told you?'

'Isn't it true?'

Enrique shrugged. '*En rigor*—strictly speaking, that is—I suppose he is right. Anyone who is involved with the land can be called a farmer. But there is much more to it than that. Much more to breeding bulls than getting a cow with calf.

And, as it happens, my father is first and foremost a businessman. He knows about growing grapes. He knows nothing about breeding bulls.'

Cassandra understood. 'But you do, right?' Her lips tightened. 'I should have known.'

Enrique gave a harsh laugh. 'Why do I get the feeling that that is not a compliment?' he asked. 'What would you know about it?'

'I know that it takes a certain kind of person to breed bulls to be slaughtered in the bullring,' retorted Cassandra, uncaring if she was overstepping the bounds of politeness. When had Enrique ever cared what he said to her? 'It's cruel, barbaric!'

Enrique sucked in a breath. 'And therefore I am cruel and barbaric also?' he suggested with dangerous civility, and Cassandra knew a twinge of fear.

'I—don't know,' she muttered, not prepared to make any accusations. Then, because she despised her cowardice, 'Are you?'

'I dare say we will find out,' he responded bleakly, his long fingers flexing on the wheel. 'Right now I am more concerned with what your son may have said to Mendoza.'

Cassandra gripped the edge of her seat. For a few shameful moments she had forgotten where she was, what she was doing here. But now the knowledge that she was soon to see her son again brought a quiver of apprehension to ferment the turmoil in her stomach.

She had never expected to come here, to see the place where Antonio had been born, where he had grown up. She had never wanted to come here, she told herself fiercely. Had never wanted to meet the family who had rejected her while her husband was alive and were rejecting her still. It was David who was welcome here. Not her.

They were driving through another valley now, a green fertile valley with a pretty village clinging to the hillside above a rocky gorge. The spire of a church rose above a stand of pine and cypress trees and the road narrowed to pass between white-walled cottages where carts and loaded mules held their own against more conventional traffic.

'What—what is this place?' Cassandra ventured, after Enrique had already acknowledged the greetings of perhaps a score of men and women, some of whom dragged wide-eyed children out of the path of the car. Older inhabitants, mostly men, she noticed, sat smoking their pipes in the shade of flower-hung balconies, and they, too, raised gnarled hands to him as he passed. 'Is—is it Tuarega?'

'It is Huerta de Tuarega,' he conceded after a moment, as if reluctant to answer her. Then, leaning towards the windscreen, he directed her gaze upward. 'There is the *palacio*.'

Palacio? Palace? Cassandra's mouth dried. The building he had indicated was situated further up the valley, surrounded by a plateau of lush fields and orchards of fruit trees. A road, its tarmac black against the terraces of olive trees that grew lower down the valley, curved away ahead of them, but it was the *palacio* itself that caused such a rush of apprehension. It looked like a sprawling medieval fortress from this angle, she thought fancifully, having never imagined anything like this. How had David ever had the nerve to come here, uninvited and unannounced?

'Does it live up to your expectations?' enquired Enrique mockingly beside her, and she turned to give him a startled look.

'I didn't have any expectations.' She swallowed. 'I—I had no idea you lived in a—in a palace.'

'No?' He was sardonic. 'But Antonio must have told you where he lived, no?'

'Yes.' Cassandra automatically adopted a defensive attitude. 'He told me his family had an estate called Tuarega. In England, estates can be large or small. They're rarely controlled from a—a palace!'

Enrique gave her a considering stare. Then, apparently deciding to give her the benefit of the doubt, he shrugged. '*Muy bien.* I believe you. But do not be alarmed. *Palacios* in Spain are not so rare. And Tuarega is really only a country house.'

Cassandra reserved judgement. Whatever Tuarega was, it was vastly different from anything she was used to. As they drew closer, she could make out towers and crenellations, and the unmistakable tracery of Moorish architecture.

'It—must be very old,' she said stiffly, trying to distract herself from the moment when she would have to get out of the car and go into the *palacio*, and Enrique inclined his head.

'Some of it is, certainly,' he agreed. 'But over the years there have been modifications and additions, so that now it is—how would you say it?—a mish-mash of styles.'

Cassandra wouldn't have said that. She wouldn't have described something that was essentially so beautiful in quite those terms. Whatever its period, Tuarega was a home to be proud of, and for all his deprecating words she sensed that deep down Enrique felt that way, too.

The sight of a herd of cattle grazing in the pasture that adjoined the formal gardens of the *palacio* briefly diverted her. The beasts raised their heads to watch the car go by, and she guessed that these were some of the fighting bulls they had been talking about. Strong, sturdy, with dangerously sharp horns, they didn't look like the domestic cattle she had seen at home and she had no desire to get any closer to them.

If Enrique noticed her unwilling interest, he made no comment. For which she was grateful. Right now, she had other things to face, to contend with, and she was glad she hadn't known exactly what she was getting into when they'd left Punta del Lobo or she might never have had the nerve to come.

But she would, she chided herself impatiently. David was here. Her son was here. And, for all its size and magnificence, Tuarega was a place where Antonio had lived.

CHAPTER SIX

THE boy came running to meet them as they entered the arched foyer of the *palacio*. Sunlight was slanting down through the grilled windows set high on the walls, throwing a barred pattern across the marble-tiled floor. David's rubber-soled shoes squeaked as he came to an abrupt halt some distance from them. Clearly, he hadn't expected to see his mother, and Enrique wondered, not without some irritation, whether the child had any thought for her feelings at all.

'Mum!' he said, his mouth tilting down at the corners. Then, twisting his gaze to her companion, his expression changed. 'Tio Enrique!' He was evidently proud of his pronunciation and he gave his uncle a delighted smile. 'I've been waiting to see you.'

Cassandra said nothing, and the awkward silence that followed his outburst was broken only by the appearance of an older man behind him. Enrique guessed Mendoza had been indulging in a little *siesta* and he evidently hadn't expected his charge to come rushing to greet them. Maybe he'd not heard the car, but David's ears were younger, and sharper, and in this place the sound of an engine could be heard for miles.

'Señor,' he exclaimed, with some humility. '*Lo siento mucho. El niño—*'

'*No importa, Carlos.*' Enrique broke into the man's apologies with a reassuring smile. 'Naturally, David is eager to speak to his mother; to apologise for his behaviour, *sin duda*. Is that not so, David?'

He arched a warning brow and the boy, clearly disconcerted by this turn of events, pulled a sulky face. 'You don't understand,' he protested, glancing defiantly towards his mother. '*She* was going to take me away.'

'We do not say ''she'' when we are speaking of our mothers,' Enrique reproved him sharply, even though the boy's words had only confirmed his suspicions about Cassandra's intentions. If he hadn't turned up at the *pensión* as he had, he might well have found himself compelled to employ a private investigator to find her. He breathed deeply and then added, 'How did you get here?'

David's chin jutted. 'Didn't *she* tell you?' he asked insolently, in deliberate contravention of his uncle's words. Then, when this didn't provoke the reaction he'd expected, he muttered sullenly, 'I got a lift.'

'A lift!' Cassandra spoke for the first time, her consternation evident. 'From Ortegar?'

'Where else?' This wasn't going at all the way David had expected and Enrique wondered what he would have done if he'd been here when the boy arrived. Taken him back to his mother, probably, he conceded drily. He had no desire to be accused of kidnapping. 'The Kaufmans weren't interested in what I did,' David continued. 'They dumped Horst on me and then cleared off to the bar.'

'That's not true.' Cassandra cast a shocked look at Enrique before chastising her son. 'Besides, you like being with Horst. You've played together all holiday.'

'All holiday!' David mimicked her. 'We've only been here for four days, Mum! And who said I liked him? He's a wimp.'

'Well, you were keen enough to go out with him and his parents this morning,' she cried, and David pulled a face.

'Haven't you figured out why?'

'That will do.' Enrique decided he had heard enough. 'Your mother asked you a question earlier. How did you get from Ortegar to Tuarega?'

'I answered her,' exclaimed David defensively, but Enrique was beginning to understand that Cassandra might well have her hands full with this young tyrant.

'To say you got a lift is not an answer,' he retorted coldly. 'From whom did you get this lift? I assume it was not with someone you knew?'

David shrugged. 'I know him now,' he said. Then, meeting Enrique's dark accusing eyes, he hunched his shoulders. 'Oh, all right. He was a wagon driver, yeah? Big deal! He even spoke English almost as well as you do. We talked about England's chances of qualifying for the World Cup.'

'Oh, David!'

Cassandra was clearly horrified and Enrique knew a quite inappropriate urge to comfort her. The boy was here, after all, safe and sound. Whatever risks he had taken, and however he deserved to be punished, she should not blame herself for his behaviour.

'I suppose the Kaufmans came moaning to you because I'd gone missing.' David was apparently unrepentant. Then, on a different tack, 'I thought you swore you'd never come here.'

'You wish,' said Cassandra tightly, recovering a little of her spirit. 'Have you any idea how worried I've been about you?'

'Oh, Mum!' David pushed his hands into the pockets of his shorts and scuffed his feet against the veined tiles. 'You must have guessed where I'd gone. Why else did you get in touch with—with him?'

He jerked his thumb towards his uncle and Enrique was amazed to discover that he badly wanted to take this young man in hand.

'Your mother did not have to get in touch with me,' he stated crisply. 'As a matter of fact, we had lunch together, and it was not until we got back to the *pensión* that we discovered you had disappeared. Or so the Kaufmans assumed. Without prior knowledge, they had no way of knowing where you had gone.'

David had listened to this statement with steadily increasing indignation, however. 'You had lunch together?' he cried accusingly. 'Why wasn't I told you were going to see one another again?'

Enrique gave him a half-amused, half-disbelieving look. 'I beg your pardon?'

'David—'

Cassandra tried to intervene, but her son was far too full of resentment to listen to her. 'I would have liked to have had lunch with you,' he exclaimed petulantly. 'Yesterday, you said you wanted to see me again. You were angry because Mum wouldn't listen to you. I bet that was why she sent me off with the Kaufmans. Just to get me out of the way.'

'David!' said Cassandra again, and Enrique couldn't let her defend herself alone.

'*Eres una—*' he began, and then cut himself off before he said something he would regret. 'The world does not revolve around you, *niño,*' he said instead. 'What your mother and I do is nothing to do with you. Do you understand me? You will never again question her actions or mine.'

David looked as if he would have liked to challenge him, but he evidently thought better of it. Dragging his feet, he moved closer to his mother, before saying sullenly, 'I want to go back to the hotel.'

Cassandra was clearly at a loss for words, and once again Enrique intervened. 'Not yet,' he said flatly. 'Your mother is tired. She needs some refreshment. I suggest we all adjourn to the patio. I will ask Consuela to bring us some iced tea.'

'I don't like iced tea,' muttered David, nudging his mother's arm. 'Can't we go? I don't like it here.'

Enrique realised that Cassandra was in a cleft stick. On the one hand she was probably relieved that he had exploded the boy's myth of a fairy godfather, but on the other she must know that giving David his own way wasn't going to do her any favours either.

'Shall I ask Consuela to attend to the matter of the refreshments?' suggested Mendoza, in his own language, and Enrique gave him an affirmative nod.

'*Gracias, Carlos,*' he agreed, then gestured towards the gallery that led to the courtyard at the back of the house. 'Will you come this way, Cassandra?'

He wasn't absolutely sure of what her reaction would be, but David grabbed her arm. 'I don't want to stay here,' he protested. 'Can't we get a taxi or something?'

'I, myself, will take you back to the *pensión* later,' essayed Enrique firmly. 'Cassandra?'

She was obviously torn two ways, but Enrique was not used to being thwarted by a nine-year-old child. 'Do not be so selfish, David,' he said, more pleasantly than he would have liked.

'You wanted to come here. Not your mother. It is only fair that you allow her to see a little of the place where your father was born and raised.'

David wouldn't look at him. 'Please, Mum,' he appealed. 'This place is old and creepy. Let's go home.'

Cassandra hesitated. Then, meeting Enrique's eyes, she said, 'Your—uncle is right. You were the one who wanted to come here, David. You can't expect to have it all your own way.'

'You would say that!' David was furious now. 'You don't care about me at all.'

'Por el amor de Dios!' Enrique's patience was at an end. 'I am beginning to doubt that you are a de Montoya, after all. Can you not show your mother some respect?'

David's eyes filled with tears, proving that for all his sulky belligerence he was still just a child at heart. 'Are—are you going to let—him—speak to me like that?' he asked tremulously, and Enrique waited with resignation for Cassandra's reply. Surely this was the opportunity she had been waiting for. And he had given it to her.

'Where did you say we could have tea?' she enquired instead, meeting Enrique's cynical gaze with searching eyes. 'I—should like a drink, if it's not too much trouble.'

He knew a fleeting sense of the initiative being taken from him, a disturbing pang of something that might have been pain in the pit of his stomach. *Caray*, but she never failed to disconcert him. And what was he doing, inviting her to have tea with him, when only the day before he had wanted to hurt her, to inflict a little of the pain on her that she had caused his family—*caused him*?

His momentary lapse meant his tone was cooler than it might have been when he said, 'Follow me,' and led the way along the vaulted gallery to the central courtyard at the back of the *palacio*.

Immediately, the beauty of his surroundings soothed him. At this hour of the afternoon, with long shadows providing welcome oases of shade beyond the shadows cast by the colonnade, the courtyard was a peaceful place. It was where his father used to sit in the late afternoon also, and Enrique had only recently come to appreciate its tranquillity after an exhausting day at the winery.

'What a—beautiful place!'

It was Cassandra who had spoken, surprising him by walking past him to admire the pool where the sound of running water was a constant delight. She rested her hands on the rim of the fountain, leaning forward to inhale the perfume from the lilies, and Enrique was instantly aware of the way the action caused her khaki shorts to ride up the backs of her legs.

Such long legs, he noticed unwillingly, as he had noticed once before, slim and shapely through the calves and thighs, deliciously rounded at the curve of her bottom—

Dios!

He turned abruptly away, half afraid that the boy who was still hanging behind him might have noticed his distraction. This was the woman who only yesterday he'd assured himself he hated. How could he look at her now with such passion when he knew what she had done to him, to his family? He must be mad!

Thankfully David had noticed nothing amiss. He was intent on kicking the fallen petals of a blossom he had found lying at his feet and Enrique felt a rekindling of the sympathy he'd felt towards his nephew the previous day. He must not lose sight of the real victim here. And it was certainly not Cassandra.

The appearance of a plump woman carrying a tray aided his recovery. '*Gracias, Consuela,*' he thanked her, after she had set her burden down on the table. Then, in her own language, 'I will let you know if we need anything else.'

'*Sí, señor.*'

Consuela, whom he'd known would be curious about the visitors, cast a startled glance at David as she withdrew, and Enrique resigned himself to the fact that any decision he might have made concerning the boy had essentially been taken out of his hands. It was one thing to trust Mendoza to keep his mouth shut and quite another to expect the woman who had been here since he and Antonio were children to remain silent about what she'd seen.

But he'd known that, he acknowledged, his eyes drifting once again towards the fountain. He'd known exactly what would happen when he'd suggested that Cassandra should stay. He would have to think seriously about what he was going to tell his mother before any rumour of the boy's identity reached her ears.

Cassandra turned then and came back to where the table was situated in the shade of the balcony, and Enrique made an effort not to stare at her. But, *Dios*, it was hard not to. Her hair was a tawny halo of red-gold curls that tumbled carelessly about her shoulders. It was longer than it had been ten years before, but just as fiery in the sunlight. He recalled how soft it had felt between his fingers—how surprised he'd been to discover in her nakedness that the colour was natural...

He hid the emotion that twisted his face by staring down at the tray Consuela had brought. Such thoughts were anathema to him, an affront to himself and his memories of his brother, and he despised himself for them. *De acuerdo*, she had not yet been married to Antonio when he'd known her, but that had been only a formality. It was no excuse for what he'd done.

Yet, she had still been a virgin...

'The village looks so small from here,' she murmured, clearly as discomfited by the situation as he was, but at least her words dispelled his painful introspection.

'Are you thirsty?' he asked, adopting a polite expression for David's sake, if nothing else. He indicated the tall glasses of iced tea with their delicate lacing of lemon slices. *'Por favor!'*

Cassandra glanced at him warily. 'I am a little thirsty,' she conceded, but he noticed that when she took the glass he offered she made sure she didn't touch his fingers with hers.

Well, that was as it should be, he told himself grimly, a pulse jerking in his temple nevertheless. Bringing her here had not been the wisest thing he'd ever done, on several counts, and he had to believe that it was the ever-present reminders of his brother that were making him so aware of his faults and hers. All the same—

'May I have a cola?' asked David at his elbow, and he

realised that the boy had come to join them. Thanks to Carlos, no doubt, there were several cans of the popular soda on the tray, the metal running with condensation in the heat.

'*Por supuesto,*' he said absently, his mind still involved with what he had been thinking. And then, realising the boy didn't understand him, he changed it to, 'Of course.' He lifted a can and flipped the tab before handing it to him. 'There you are.'

'Thanks.' David took the can, but instead of drinking from it he bit his lip. 'I'm—sorry, Uncle Enrique,' he said. 'Sorry I was thoughtless, I mean.' He cast his mother a rueful glance. 'I didn't mean to worry you, Mum.'

Cassandra looked taken aback and Enrique guessed David wasn't always as willing to back down. 'We'll talk about it later,' she said quickly, taking refuge in her glass. Then, with an obvious effort to be civil, she licked a pearl of moisture from her lip and added, 'This is delicious. Iced tea never tastes like this back home.'

Which was as good as saying she would talk to David when they were alone, Enrique conceded drily. This whole situation was rapidly losing any credibility at all. *Dios*, what did she think she was doing here? How was she going to justify what had happened to herself? Sooner or later she would have to accept that there was no alternative. One way or another, Enrique and his father were going to have a role in David's life.

David had moved away now, carrying his soda across to the fountain that his mother had been admiring earlier, and Enrique moved closer to Cassandra. 'I spoke to my mother last evening,' he said, forcing her to look up at him. She shouldn't imagine that because David was here he wouldn't say what he thought. He'd tried talking to her earlier in the day and that had not been a success. She had to be made to see that avoiding the issue was going to achieve nothing.

'Really?' she said now, and he knew a moment's regret when he saw the guarded look in her eyes. It was obvious she was still not prepared to compromise with him, despite what had happened. Her spine was very stiff as she continued, 'Is that supposed to mean something to me?'

Enrique took a deep breath. 'She told me that my father is making good progress,' he said evenly. He didn't add that she'd been put out by his failure to ring her at the time he'd promised or that he'd mentioned nothing about what he'd been doing all day. 'She hopes he will be able to return home in a matter of days.'

Cassandra lifted her slim shoulders. 'I'm happy for you.'

'Are you?' Enrique felt a quite compulsive desire to shock her. 'Why? Because it means David will get to know his grandparents that much sooner?'

A hand fluttered to her throat and, for all her efforts to appear composed, he could see the fear she was trying so hard to hide. 'You are joking?'

'I do not make jokes, Cassandra.' Enrique despised the wave of sympathy she aroused in him, and his words were unnecessarily harsh as he added, 'You are fighting a losing battle. Admit it. The boy has shown how he feels about it. All right, perhaps his method of achieving his ends left a lot to be desired. I accept that. But you are not going to get anywhere if you insist on denying him his right to know his Spanish family.'

Cassandra swallowed. He saw the way the muscles in her throat worked to hide the emotion she was fighting. Then, setting her glass down on the tray, she said tightly, 'Will you allow me to ring for a taxi to take us back to Punta del Lobo?'

Enrique sighed. 'I have told you: I will take you back to the *pensión* myself. There is no need for you to call a taxi.'

She shook her head. 'I would prefer to.'

'And can you afford it?'

His words were unforgivable, and he regretted them as soon as they were said. But it was too late. She had heard him, and his careless tongue aroused her as a polite denial would never have done.

'Of course, I would expect you to say something like that,' she told him in a low scornful voice. 'That is all you care about, isn't it? You and your father both. That was why you were so against me marrying Antonio, wasn't it? Because I didn't have any money. Because in your world having no money equals gold-digger, right? Well, you know what? I'd rather possess a poverty of the wallet than one of the spirit!'

She was staring at him now, her eyes wide and filled with righteous outrage. Dark lashes, unmistakably damp with tears, shaded pupils that were an incredible shade of blue, and he felt their condemnation in every pore of his being. For the first time in his life he was aware of his own arrogance, of the cynicism that had coloured all his dealings with this woman. And for the first time, also, he felt himself to be at not only an emotional but a psychological disadvantage, too.

'*Lo siento,*' he found himself saying softly. 'I am sorry. I should not have said what I did.' He paused. 'Will you forgive me?'

Cassandra rubbed the end of her nose with her knuckle. 'Do you care?' she demanded with a sniff, and before he could prevent it his hands had reached out to grip her arms just above her elbows.

It was a mistake. Her skin was like satin, soft and warm and deliciously sensitive to the touch. He knew that any pressure he brought to bear would leave dark bruises on her flesh and, for an insane moment, he wanted to do just that. To put his mark on her; to have the rest of the world see exactly what he'd done.

It was insane. He knew that. But that didn't stop him from feeling as he did. His eyes searched her face, wanting to see some matching emotion in hers, and settled on the parted fullness of her mouth. It was wide and sweet, her tongue hovering nervously over her lower lip, and for one mindless moment he wanted to touch it, to taste it, to allow his tongue to probe deeply into that hot moist cavern...

But it didn't happen. Although he was sure Cassandra was aware of the unexpected intimacy between them, she didn't respond as he had. With a muffled cry, she wrenched herself away from him, and David, who had been casting nervously surreptitious glances at them from the safety of the pool, now came awkwardly back to his mother's side.

'What's wrong?' he asked, his dark eyes, so like Enrique's own, moving from his mother to his uncle and back again.

'You're not still mad, are you, Mum? I was afraid you weren't going to let me see Uncle Enrique again, that's all.'

But that wasn't all, thought Enrique grimly, struggling to regain a sense of balance. Touching Cassandra had briefly torn aside the veneer of indifference that had sustained him. He'd forgotten how soft her skin was, how seductively feminine was her scent. For a few crazy seconds he'd wanted her to remember how it had once been between them without considering how dangerously attractive such a memory might be to himself.

Now, however, he had to reassure the boy, and, putting the destructive knowledge of his own weakness aside, he said harshly, 'Your mother knows there is no way she can prevent you from meeting the rest of your family.' He looked at Cassandra now with challenging eyes. 'Is that not so?' And when she didn't reply, he added, 'We will discuss this again tomorrow, no? When you have had time to recover from the shock of David's disappearance.'

CHAPTER SEVEN

ENRIQUE arrived as Cassandra was having breakfast the next morning.

Well, calling several cups of strong black coffee breakfast was pushing it a little, she conceded, but after the events of the past few days her appetite was practically non-existent.

She had certainly been in no mood for dinner the night before and although she'd taken David, at his suggestion, to a local pizzeria, she had had a struggle swallowing more than a few mouthfuls of her pasta.

David had been on his best behaviour, of course. He'd spent the first hour apologising for worrying her and the Kaufmans, and when he'd seen the German family later in the evening, he'd made a point of speaking to them personally. She didn't know what exactly he'd said to them. She told herself she didn't want to know. His attitude was far too reminiscent of his father and how charming he had been when he'd wanted his own way.

Nevertheless, David had got his own way and they both knew it. Whatever Cassandra said now, whatever she did, she had the weight of the de Montoyas' involvement hanging over her, and she wouldn't have been human if she hadn't felt betrayed in some way.

Yet, despite her misgivings, she couldn't prevent the thrill of recognition she felt when Enrique appeared in the doorway to the terrace, his eyes swiftly scanning its occupants in search of herself. Or in search of David, she amended bitterly. She had to remember this man was David's friend, not hers.

All the same, she was intensely aware of him. His tall dark figure, dressed more formally this morning in a pale grey button-down shirt and black trousers, was undeniably striking. And when he located her table beside the rail of the terrace and started towards her, his progress was monitored by more than one pair of curious eyes.

Cassandra felt the colour rise up her throat as he stopped beside her table. *'Puedo?'* he asked, which she thought meant, May I? But he didn't wait for her permission before pulling out the chair opposite, swinging it round and straddling it with his long legs.

She was immediately conscious of the fact that she hadn't bothered to put on any make-up that morning. Not that she wore a lot. But she usually used an eyeliner and a lipstick because of her fair colouring. However, with David still asleep, she'd merely sluiced her face in the tiny bathroom that adjoined their room and pulled on the tee shirt and knee-length trousers she'd worn the evening before.

'You're very early,' she said, unconsciously defensive. 'David isn't up yet.'

'It is not David I wish to speak to,' replied Enrique, before glancing round for a waiter. With enviable ease, he summoned the man and ordered coffee for himself, even though Cassandra was sure the little *pensión* didn't normally cater to visitors. Then, meeting her unwilling gaze with his own, 'Did you sleep well?'

Cassandra pushed nervous fingers through her hair. 'I suppose that's a polite way of saying I look a mess,' she declared, stiffening her spine. 'What do you want, Enrique?'

'I want to speak with you.' The waiter returned with his coffee and he pulled a note out of his pocket and pressed it into the startled man's hand with a quick, *'Gracias!'* Then, facing her again he added, 'Do not be so anxious, Cassandra. This need not be as unpleasant as you fear.'

'Want to bet?'

Cassandra's response was muffled as she looked down at her cup but he heard her. 'I mean it,' he said. 'It can be hard or easy. It is up to you.'

'Oh, right.' She looked up then. 'As long as I let you do exactly as you like, I'll find it easy. If I object, you'll fight me.' Her lips twisted. 'What a choice!'

Enrique shook his head. 'I do not want to fight you, Cassandra.'

'But you will if you have to.'

'If you attempt to deny my father the right to meet his grandson, I must.'

Cassandra made a scornful sound. 'And that's supposed to reassure me?'

Enrique drew a deep breath. 'I am not your enemy, Cassandra.' His long fingers tightened on the back of the chair. 'Why can you not understand my feelings? The boy is a de Montoya. You do not deny that?' And, when she didn't protest, '*Aquí tiene*, is it not reasonable that he should have the chance to learn about his heritage?' He paused. 'At this moment, he is my father's only hope for the future. Though, of course, he does not know it yet.'

Cassandra stiffened. 'What are you saying?'

Enrique sighed. 'I should have thought it was perfectly obvious.'

Panic gripped her. 'Are—are you implying that—that David—'

'Will one day be heir to Tuarega?' Enrique finished for her. 'It is very possible, yes.'

'No!' Cassandra was appalled.

'No?' Enrique arched a dark brow. 'Why not?'

'Because you—you are your father's eldest son. It is—it is your son who will inherit Tuarega.'

'And if I do not have a son?' Enrique stared at her, his eyes enigmatic in his dark face. 'It is entirely possible. I do not intend to marry, therefore—'

'But you must.' Cassandra shook her head. 'David's my son. *Mine*. He doesn't need what—what you're offering.'

'Does he not? Can you make that decision for him?'

'No, but—' Cassandra caught her breath. 'Enrique, he's just a child!'

'I know that.' Enrique lifted his shoulders in a dismissing gesture. 'And I am not suggesting that he should be faced with such a choice until he is older. Much older. But that does not mean that he should not be given the chance to learn about his Spanish family, to avail himself of the advantages we can give him.'

Cassandra shook her head. 'You can't do this.'

But they could, and she knew it. Had always known it, if she was honest. She'd told herself that Antonio's family didn't deserve to know about David, but what she'd really been doing was saving herself from further heartbreak.

'I want him to come and stay at Tuarega,' continued Enrique levelly. 'I think he should spend the rest of his holiday there.'

'You're not serious!' Cassandra stared at him disbelievingly. 'You have to give me some time—'

'For what?' Enrique's eyes were wary. 'To poison his mind against me?'

'No.' She would never do that. 'But it's too soon.'

'I disagree.' Enrique was implacable. 'It is the most sensible solution. He will enjoy it.' He paused. 'You both will.'

'Both?' Cassandra's jaw dropped. 'You expect me to come with him?'

'I am not entirely inhuman, no matter what you think of me,' replied Enrique flatly. 'I am not suggesting taking the boy away from you. That was never my intention. But perhaps it is time to put the past behind us.'

Cassandra couldn't think. 'We can't do that.'

'Perhaps not.' He had the grace to look slightly discomfited now. '*No haga este!* Do not do this, Cassandra.' He pushed his untouched coffee cup aside. 'Be reasonable, I beg you.'

'As you are?' Cassandra made a helpless gesture. Then, 'All right,' she said heavily. 'Ask David if he wants to spend the rest of his holiday at Tuarega. I can't stop you. But don't expect me to go with you.'

'Cassandra!' His use of her name was anguished, and she glanced anxiously about her, half afraid their conversation was being monitored, too. 'When are you going to realise that what is done cannot be undone? I did not write that letter. David did. Can you not try and understand how he feels?'

Cassandra couldn't look at him. 'David's a child,' she persisted. 'What makes you think he'll want to go to Tuarega? What is there for him? He gets bored very easily.'

'Does he?' Enrique considered her words. 'Well, you may be right. There is no beach at Tuarega, it is true. No shops or fast-food restaurants within walking distance.'

'David isn't interested in shopping,' Cassandra admitted unwillingly. 'But he does like the beach. He likes to swim.'

'*Bien.*' Enrique was philosophic. 'We do have a swimming pool, *por lo menos*. That may be some compensation.'

And, of course, it would be. Cassandra had to be honest with herself. Not to mention the fact that there was space at Tuarega; acres and acres of space, grazed by Enrique's bulls and probably horses, too. David could swim; he might even learn to ride. He would begin to appreciate how much she had deprived him of.

Cassandra's stomach hollowed. What Enrique and his father had to offer was overwhelming, *terrifying*. How could she hope to compete with the wealth and influence of the de Montoyas? Her son was too young to understand what she had had to pay for that wealth and influence.

'It is time you met your in-laws, too,' continued Enrique persuasively. 'My father has mellowed somewhat in his old age. When he learns about David, he will not turn you away.'

'Won't he?'

Cassandra wished she could believe him. Considering the lengths to which Julio de Montoya had gone to ensure that the wedding between her and his younger son did not take place, Enrique's words did not fill her with any degree of optimism. Besides, she wasn't at all sure she wanted to meet the man who had attempted—with his son's help—to ruin her life.

Even so, she couldn't deny that Enrique had a point. Perhaps she was being selfish in attempting to deprive David of the chance to choose between them. Just because she had suffered at the hands of the de Montoyas there was no reason to believe that her son would.

'I promise I will see that you—and David—enjoy your stay in my family home,' declared Enrique, watching her with his intent dark eyes, and she shivered. 'Please: say you will come.'

*   *   *

Enrique was in his father's study when Sanchia de Silvestre de Romero was announced.

Squashing the immediate sense of irritation he felt at her appearance at this time, he abandoned the schedule he'd been working on and got to his feet as Consuela showed the young woman into the room.

As always, Sanchia looked sleek and sophisticated, her dark hair coiled into a chignon at the nape of her neck, her sleeveless sheath fairly screaming its designer label. But today, for some reason, he found her appearance far too formal for a casual visit, and he wished she had rung before turning up like this.

'You will not believe it, *querido*!' she exclaimed, apparently unaware of the tension in his expression. She waited until Consuela had withdrawn, closing the door behind her, and then circled the desk to where he stood, reaching up to bestow a lingering kiss against his taut cheek. 'Do you know, your man, Mendoza, stopped me in the *salón* and asked me if I was expected? Such insolence! I told him I did not need an appointment to see *mi amante*, no?'

Enrique gave a small smile. But it was an effort, nonetheless. 'Carlos is aware that I am extremely busy, Sanchia,' he said, irrationally annoyed by her familiarity. He was not her lover. They had slept together a handful of times as much at her behest as his. 'Unless it is something urgent, I regret I will have to ask you to excuse me.'

Sanchia's lower lip jutted. 'You are sending me away? Again?'

Enrique stifled a sigh. 'I am sorry. As I say, I am very busy, Sanchia. I have to go to Sevilla this evening, to see my father, and there are things that must be done before I leave.'

Sanchia gazed at him. 'But Consuela says you have guests at the *palacio*. Surely you are not going to Sevilla and leaving your guests alone?'

Enrique bent his head so that Sanchia wouldn't see his exasperated closing of his eyes. He would have to speak to Consuela, he thought impatiently. To warn her not to gossip to the Señora de Silvestre de Romero as if she were already a member of his household. Which she would never be, however much she might presume upon it.

'Who are these guests?' Sanchia went on in the same proprietary tone. 'Are they exporters, dealers, what? Have they come to see the bulls?'

'They are—family,' said Enrique reluctantly, aware that Cassandra would not approve of his description. But there seemed little point in lying about it. Sooner or later, Sanchia was going to find out who they were.

'Family?' Sanchia's eyes brightened. 'Who? Your Tia Alicia? Your cousin Sebastian and his wife? Oh, I do like your Tia Alicia. She knows so much about your family—'

'It is not Tia Alicia,' said Enrique flatly, steeling himself to tell her exactly who his visitors were, when there was a knock at the door. Guessing it was Consuela again, come to ask if they would like some refreshments, Enrique called, 'Come!' with some relief at the diversion.

His deliverance was short-lived, however. It was not Consuela who pushed open the heavy door and stepped into the room. It was David, and he gazed curiously at his uncle's visitor before saying cheerfully, 'This is some place, Uncle Enrique. It's taken me ages to find you.'

Sanchia's face was a picture of consternation, and if Enrique hadn't felt so exasperated at the boy's intrusion he might well have found the situation ludicrous. After all, he had probably looked much like her when he saw David for the first time, but he shouldn't forget that, apart from her shock at seeing the boy, Sanchia was also looking at the son of the man she herself had expected to marry.

No one spoke, and it was David who broke the uneasy silence that had fallen at his entrance. 'Did I do something wrong, Uncle Enrique?' he asked with boyish candour, and Enrique guessed he was remembering what had happened the day before. 'Um—Mum said I could come down and find you, if I wanted to.'

Did she?

Enrique didn't voice the words, but they presented themselves, nonetheless. Had Cassandra sent her son down here to embarrass him? Because if she had, she had certainly succeeded.

'Nothing is wrong, David,' he assured him now, speaking in English and realising he was being overly suspicious. It was unlikely that Cassandra—or David, for that matter—could have known of Sanchia's arrival. He had had his father's housekeeper accommodate their guests in rooms at the opposite end of the *palacio* from those occupied by the family and unless someone else had been gossiping this was just an unfortunate coincidence.

'That's all right, then.' David gave Sanchia another speculative glance but it was obvious he could hardly contain his excitement. 'I've seen the swimming pool, Uncle Enrique. It's huge!'

'*Quien—?*' It was obvious that Sanchia was having difficulty in getting her words out. '*Quien este, Enrique?* Who is this?'

'My name's David de Montoya.' Once again, the boy forestalled his uncle. 'Mum and me are going to stay here for the rest of our holidays. Isn't that great?'

Sanchia didn't answer him, but she turned uncomprehending eyes on Enrique, and he came round the desk to put a hand on his nephew's shoulder.

'He is right,' he said, speaking in English again, deciding that perhaps this was the easiest way, after all. 'David is Antonio's son.'

'*Antonio's son!*' Sanchia looked horrified. Then, in their own language, 'Antonio did not have a son.'

'Oh, but he did,' said Enrique swiftly, aware that David was listening to this exchange and must have sensed her antipathy. 'David is nine years old—*sí*, David?'

Sanchia shook her head, as if to clear it, and then returned to the offensive. 'But—how do you know that he is Antonio's son? Who told you that he is?'

'*Este seria!*' Enrique's impatience was obvious. 'Be serious, Sanchia,' he exclaimed, his eyes flashing an unmistakable message of warning. 'Have you looked at him? He is a de Montoya. He is the image of my brother at that age.'

'Or of you,' retorted Sanchia shortly. 'He bears a resemblance to both of you, but that does not mean—' She broke off, aware that she was doing herself no favours by voicing her doubts. Then, with hardly less censure, 'Do you tell me that you have invited—that woman to stay at Tuarega?' Her dismay contorted her expression. 'Enrique, have you taken leave of your senses? Do you want your father to have another heart attack? He will if he discovers you have had that—that *puta* here behind his back!'

'*Es suficiente!*' Enrique silenced her with the harsh words, aware that the anger he felt at her outburst was out of all proportion to the offence. *Dios mio*, only days ago he would have agreed with her. 'Nothing is being done behind my father's back,' he continued tightly. 'As it happens, I am going to Sevilla this evening for that very purpose. To speak to my mother. To discuss with her the best method to proceed.'

David was looking worried now. 'Something is wrong, Uncle Enrique!' he exclaimed, turning to look up at him, and for the first time Enrique saw a trace of his mother's fragility in his face. 'What are you talking about? Why is—she—so cross?'

Sanchia's nostrils flared. 'I need to speak to you alone, Enrique,' she said coldly, ignoring the boy's appeal and continuing to speak in Spanish. 'Why do you not ask—David—' Her lips thinned as if in distaste. 'Why do you not get the boy to ask Mendoza to accompany him on a tour of the *palacio*. You and I have matters to discuss.'

Enrique squeezed David's shoulder and then let him go to move back behind his desk. 'I regret I do not have the time to discuss anything at present,' he said, speaking English for the child's benefit. 'Perhaps we can continue this at another date, Sanchia.'

Sanchia's teeth ground together. 'You present me with a *fait accompli* and expect me to accept it, just like that?' she demanded. 'No apologies; no explanations. Simply the bald fact that the woman who ruined my life is staying here, with you, as a *guest*! *Dios*, Enrique, what do you think I am?'

Enrique expelled a wary breath. 'I know it must have been a shock, Sanchia—'

'A shock!' She uttered a mirthless laugh. 'If you had wanted to destroy me, you could not have chosen a better way.'

'Oh, please, Sanchia!' Enrique wished David wasn't hearing this but there was no way he could send him away without it appearing that he had indeed trespassed on his uncle's hospitality. 'Are you not being a little over-dramatic? I doubt that meeting Antonio's son is in any way destructive to your peace of mind today. It is almost ten years since my brother died.'

Sanchia gasped. 'And you think I should have forgotten how he deserted me for—for that—?'

'In the name of God, Sanchia!' Enrique lapsed into his own language to put an end to this. 'How can you expect me to believe that Antonio ruined your life when less than six months later you married Alfonso de Romero?'

Sanchia's mouth opened and closed, but no sound came out and, deciding he could not let David listen to any more of this, Enrique came round his desk again and smiled down at his nephew.

'Perhaps Señora de Romero is right, David,' he said gently. 'Do as she suggests and go and find Carlos. He will be happy to show you the rest of the *palacio*.'

David gave Sanchia a doubtful look. Then, returning his attention to his uncle, he asked, 'Will I see you again after—after Señora de Romero has gone?'

'Later,' declared Enrique firmly, propelling the boy towards the door. 'Now, go. You will find Carlos in the orangery. Do you know where that is?'

'I'll find it.' David looked a little mutinous now. 'What shall I tell Mum? Is Señora de Romero a friend of hers, too?'

Enrique was pretty sure that David knew she wasn't but he refused to get into that. Nevertheless, as he turned back to

Sanchia, he couldn't help the treacherous thought that he understood perfectly why Antonio had preferred Cassandra to Sanchia.

He always had...

CHAPTER EIGHT

CASSANDRA didn't see Enrique again that day.

According to David his uncle had gone to Seville, and Cassandra could only assume he had gone to see his father. To bring him up to date on current events? she wondered uneasily. It seemed the most likely explanation, yet Enrique had said that his father was recovering from major surgery. Did he really intend to risk his recovery by giving the old man another shock?

Or was she inventing reasons why Enrique shouldn't tell Julio de Montoya about David? After all, it was Enrique's father who called the shots at Tuarega, and, so long as the old man wasn't involved, she could still kid herself that she and her son could leave here at the end of their holiday with no harm done.

Yeah, right.

Deep inside, Cassandra knew there was no hope of that. From the moment David had devised his plan of writing to his grandfather, she had been on a collision course with Julio de Montoya. It was just a pity that it had taken weeks for her to find out about it.

David, himself, had come back from his exploration of the *palacio* full of excitement about where he'd been and what he'd seen. And, to a degree, Cassandra could understand his feelings. There was no doubt that Tuarega was the most beautiful place she had ever seen, and the rooms she and David had been given were nothing short of magnificent.

The *palacio* itself was divided into several apartments, each with its own courtyard and patio, all of which were interconnected by covered walkways or colonnades. Flowers spilled from dozens of tubs and planters, curled about the narrow white columns that supported the roof, and tumbled from balconies in exotic profusion.

Cassandra knew, because Señora de Riviera, the de Montoyas' housekeeper, had told her in heavily accented English, that Enrique and his parents occupied the main apartments that overlooked the courtyard, where they had had tea the afternoon before. But she and David had been accommodated some distance from there in a sunny pavilion with its own long reflecting pool outside, where tiny tropical fish swam amongst saucer-sized water lilies.

Cassandra wondered if their rooms had formed part of the *seraglio*, or harem, when Tuarega had been a Moorish stronghold. They were certainly set apart from the rest of the building, though the paintings and murals that adorned the walls and ceilings in her bedroom and bathroom seemed to give the lie to that supposition. Surely there was too much eroticism implicit in the images of semi-naked women bathing and anointing their bodies with what appeared to be perfumed oils to warrant that belief, but she still suspected the choice of accommodation had been a deliberate one on Enrique's part.

Nevertheless, the spacious *salón*, with its rich carpets and heavily carved furniture, was in no way inferior to the rest of the *palacio*. Some of the artwork was undoubtedly priceless, and the jewel-bright cushions that were strewn about the floors and sofas gave each room a glowing brilliance.

Adjoining the *salón* was an equally impressive dining room. Carved chairs were set about a granite-topped wrought-iron table, and a gold candelabrum supported several heavily scented black candles, giving the room a distinctly foreign ambience.

David had his own bedroom, of course, and, to his delight, his own bathroom, too. Like her own bedroom and bathroom, they were equipped with every possible convenience, which didn't make it any easier for Cassandra to face the prospect of him returning home.

The Kaufmans had been sorry when she'd told them that she and David were leaving the *pensión*. She'd felt obliged to give them an explanation after the fiasco of the day before and, although she felt sure that Franz Kaufman, at least, had put a different interpretation on her decision from the real one, she was not prepared to justify her actions to him. Let him think that she'd been as eager as her son to make contact with her Spanish in-laws, she thought. It was easier than to try and explain something which, even to her own ears, sounded very unlikely.

Señor Movida had expressed his regret at their departure. Although he would be able to re-let their rooms without too much difficulty at this time of year, he had assured her that he was going to miss her friendly face about the place. Which had touched Cassandra a little. It was good to know that someone cared.

Awakening at Tuarega the next morning did cause her some misgivings, however. Despite the fact that she and David had enjoyed a delicious supper in their own apartments last evening, and her fears that Enrique intended to monopolise her son's time had not been realised, she was not foolish enough to believe that she was going to have much say in his activities from now on. Enrique had brought them here so that David could get to know his Spanish family, his Spanish heritage. Allowing him to spend all his time with his mother was unlikely to accomplish this and she might as well accept it.

Even so, as she left her bed and trod barefoot across the cool marble tiles to the balcony that adjoined her room, Cassandra found her thoughts straying into another area. Over supper, David had admitted that his uncle had had a visitor when he'd gone to his study the previous afternoon. Ignoring her question as to whether he had been trespassing, David had gone on to explain that the visitor had been a young woman, who had been cross with his uncle for reasons he didn't understand.

They'd been speaking mostly in Spanish, he'd said, and Cassandra had been diverted from her own doubts about David's behaviour to speculate on who the young woman might be. It seemed obvious to her, if not to her son, that this woman resented their arrival, but why? Was this Enrique's girlfriend? His fiancée? Her lips twisted with unconscious irony. How she wished she could discredit him. Although she had no quarrel with the other woman, Enrique deserved a taste of his own medicine.

But it was no use wasting her time on such futile schemes. If he was engaged to this woman, it was nothing to do with her. Still, it seemed there was at least one more person to whom David's presence at Tuarega was not proving very appealing. Who was she? Cassandra wondered again, gripping the balcony rail with nervous fingers. And why did she care?

It was another beautiful morning. It was still fairly early but the sun was up, and the tiles of the balcony were already warm beneath her feet. Unlike her bedroom. She'd discovered that, although their apartments were not air-conditioned, the thickness of the walls prevented them from getting too hot. But out here, with the sun shining down out of a cloudless sky, she did not have any protection.

There seemed to be few people about that she could see. In the distance, beyond the jasmine-covered grille that edged the patio, a man was working in the gardens that surrounded the *palacio*, and somewhere the steady drone of a lawnmower broke the stillness. Even so, she was suddenly conscious of the scarcity of her attire—the oversized tee shirt she used to sleep in exposing far too much thigh for her liking—and, deciding to go and find her son, she abandoned the balcony in favour of her bedroom.

When she ventured into David's room, however, she found her son was gone. His bed had been slept in: the tumbled sheets were evidence of that. But his sleeping shorts lay discarded on the floor and, when she checked, she found the clothes he'd worn the day before had disappeared.

Cassandra sighed. She wasn't worried exactly. It was unlikely he'd ventured far from the *palacio*, and there were any number of staff around to see that he came to no harm. All the same, she couldn't help feeling a bit disappointed that he hadn't told her where he was going. This was their first day here, after all, and he should know she was as anxious as he was to get her bearings.

There was no point in stressing over it, however, and, going back to her own room, Cassandra took a quick shower before getting dressed. But, as she surveyed the clothes she'd brought with her, she couldn't help wishing she'd packed more summer dresses. Not that she had an extensive wardrobe, of course, but she had left several cotton dresses at home in favour of shorts and cut-offs, and cropped shirts of one sort or another.

She eventually decided to wear knee-length trousers in a soft cream micro-fibre with one of her less skimpy tops tucked firmly into the waistband. Then, securing her hair in a ponytail, she thrust her feet into heelless pumps and left her room.

Finding her way back to the main part of the *palacio* was not so easy, however. Accompanying Señora de Riviera along these corridors the previous day, Cassandra had been too overwhelmed by the beauty of her surroundings to pay a lot of attention to their actual direction. It was not until she emerged into another sunlit courtyard that she had to acknowledge that she was lost.

Crossing the paved path that circled another pool, this one with its own ornate fountain spilling water into a marble basin, she walked to the edge of the courtyard and looked out over a fertile landscape. Below her, the ground fell away gradually to the valley floor, wide terraces providing room for the acres of what she surmised were orange trees, judging by the overpowering scent of citrus that filled her nose. She wondered how many trees there were. Hundreds, certainly; possibly even thousands. But they were just a small part of the estate that was Tuarega, and she was reminded of how unreal her presence here seemed.

'What are you doing?'

Enrique's voice startled her, and she glanced round almost guiltily to find him standing beside the fountain. She hadn't heard his approach. She'd been too intent on her thoughts. And it was disconcerting to find him there, lean and dark and somehow menacing, watching her.

'I—got lost,' she admitted, deciding there was no point in lying about it. 'I was looking for David and—well, I seem to have missed my way.'

'Ah.' Enrique inclined his head and strolled towards her, not stopping until he, too, could see down into the valley. 'Are you admiring my father's fruit trees?'

'I was trying to estimate how many there were,' Cassandra conceded, pushing her hands into the back pockets of her trousers and lifting her shoulders in an awkward gesture. 'Are oranges easy to grow?'

'Comparatively so,' agreed Enrique, his dark eyes cool and assessing. 'They have their problems, as do we all. The fruit fly has not been totally eradicated, and a good grower is always alert for any pest which might damage his crop.' His lips tightened. 'Are you really interested, Cassandra? Or is this simply a way of avoiding the obvious?'

'The obvious?' Cassandra wasn't entirely sure she knew what he meant. 'You mean David? Do you know where he is?'

'He is with Juan Martinez, my chief stockman,' said Enrique at once. 'He came out to the paddocks this morning as we were examining the new calves.' He paused, and then went on slowly, 'It was not an entirely sensible thing to do. These cattle are not like your English domestic breeds. They have moods, temperament. An abundance of spirit. Without proper supervision, it is easy to see how accidents can happen.'

Cassandra's throat dried. 'Are you telling me that David was in danger? That these animals are killers?'

'No.'

'But you are. Or at least that's what you implied.'

'I said, entering the paddocks without giving any thought to what he might be getting into was reckless,' amended Enrique patiently. 'Contrary to popular belief, bulls do not attack without provocation.'

'So you say.' But Cassandra was dismayed. 'I think it's appalling!'

A muscle in Enrique's jaw jerked. 'Exactly what do you find appalling?' he asked harshly, and Cassandra knew a sudden sense of alarm. 'Me?'

'Of course not.' Though she wasn't being totally truthful.

'I meant breeding—breeding animals to be slaughtered in the bullring.' She took a breath. 'You know how I feel about it. I told you the other day.'

'And what exactly do you think your English farmers do with the bulls they breed?' he demanded, stepping closer to her, and Cassandra felt the heat rise up her face. It was hot outdoors, but it was an inner heat that was lifting her temperature, beading her upper lip with moisture, causing a rivulet of perspiration to funnel down between her breasts.

'That's—different,' she declared staunchly, lifting a protective hand to her throat.

His eyes darkened. 'How is it different?'

'Because—because they're slaughtered for food.'

'Really?' Enrique regarded her intently, so close now she could feel the heat of his body, too. 'And you think that killing beasts before they're half grown is acceptable, *sí*?'

'People eat beef. They're bred for a purpose.'

'And so are my bulls,' Enrique informed her flatly. 'Plus the fact that a bull is already four years old before he enters the bullring. A more reasonable lifespan than—what? Eighteen months or so?'

Cassandra shifted her weight from one foot to the other. 'You have your opinion. I have mine.'

'Ah, yes.' Enrique regarded her from beneath lowered lids. 'But you do not think my opinion matters, do you, Cassandra? And we are not just talking about my bulls, here.'

'What do you want me to say?' Cassandra spoke quickly, wishing she could put some distance between them. But he had trapped her between his body and the trellis of flowering vines behind her that edged the courtyard and she was intensely aware of how vulnerable she was. 'We're here, aren't we? You can hardly claim that that was my decision.'

'No.'

He conceded the point, but he continued to regard her in such a way that a spark of real fear ignited inside her. He was so powerful, so disturbing; so male. And what she was most afraid of was her own unwanted awareness of him as a man. She could remember too well how abandoned he had once made her feel. How helpless; how eager; and ultimately how ashamed...

'This is not an easy situation for any of us,' he continued at last, his mouth acquiring a dangerously indulgent softness. 'We share too many memories, you and I.' He lifted his hand and, to her dismay, he stroked a long mocking finger down her cheek and along her jawline. 'Couldn't you at least try and understand my feelings?'

Cassandra jerked her head away from his questing touch, rushing into speech to destroy the sudden intimacy between them. 'I—I don't know what—what you expect me to—to do,' she stammered wildly, desperate to get away from him. 'I— I'm sorry if our being here is putting a strain on your love-life, but I—that's not my fault—'

'What did you say?' His harsh response banished any pretence of understanding. With anger darkening his expression he reached for her, one hand circling her upper arm, the other curling about her nape and jerking her towards him. He thrust his face close to hers. 'What are you talking about?'

Cassandra was shocked out of her inertia. 'Oh, please,' she cried, trying futilely to prise his fingers from her arm. 'You know what I'm talking about. David saw you with her yesterday afternoon. He said she wasn't very impressed to see him.'

Enrique ignored her efforts to try and free herself. 'Saw me with whom?' he demanded grimly, apparently uncaring that he was embracing her in full view of anyone who cared to walk along the upper landing of the building that surrounded them on three sides. From a distance, no one would know his true feelings. 'Talk to me, Cassandra. Tell me who you think she was.'

Cassandra felt impotent. 'I don't know who she was, do I?' she exclaimed. 'You don't share your secrets with me.'

'No,' he agreed harshly. 'But you are prepared to speculate, are you not?'

'Enrique—'

'I will tell you, she is not my—what would you say? My girlfriend, *sí*? Her name is Sanchia, Cassandra. Sanchia de

Romero. She is the woman my brother was going to marry before he became—before he met you!'

Cassandra swallowed. 'I—I don't believe you.'

'Why would I lie?'

Why indeed?

Cassandra gazed up into his dark face with troubled eyes, the idea that Antonio's ex-fiancée was still a regular visitor in this house filling her with dismay. 'I—didn't know,' she excused herself lamely, wishing she hadn't spoken so impulsively, and Enrique's mouth compressed into a thin line.

'There is a lot you do not know, Cassandra,' he told her grimly, but he was looking at her differently now, his expression taut with suppressed emotion. 'Do you think you are the only one of us who has any feelings at all?'

Cassandra couldn't speak, couldn't move, couldn't drag her eyes away from his. A moment before she had been afraid of his anger; now she was afraid of herself. His hand about her arm wasn't hurting her any more. It abraded her flesh with an entirely sensual movement, his fingers at her nape flexing against her skin.

His thumb found the tender hollow below her ear and a pulse leapt nervously beneath his touch. Her shallow breathing couldn't prevent her breasts from brushing constantly against his chest, her nipples hardening to pebbles beneath the cloth of her sleeveless shirt. His thigh had parted her legs in an effort to keep his balance, and every nerve in her body felt as if it was on red alert. She could feel herself succumbing to his sexuality, her body weakening instinctively in response to his.

'This is not wise,' he said roughly, his eyes moving almost compulsively to her mouth, and she realised he was as aware of what was happening as she was.

'Then let me go,' she pleaded unsteadily, though she made no attempt to move away. And Enrique sensed that she was susceptible to this sudden intimacy between them. It was evident in the dark fire that blazed suddenly in his eyes.

'I will,' he said savagely, but his actions belied his words. His head dipped until his lips were only a few inches away from hers, his breath warm and sensual. 'I must,' he added barely audibly before he bent even lower and touched her mouth with his.

The fire that erupted between them was as uncontrollable as it was instantaneous. As it had been once before, Cassandra recalled in her last lucid moments before the hungry ardour of his kiss drove all other thoughts out of her head. Hardly aware of what she was doing, she gave in to the needs she'd been fighting ever since she'd encountered Enrique again on the forecourt of the *pensión*. Needs that involved clutching his warm neck with her fingers, burrowing closer to him, easing her aching nipples against the muscled hardness of his chest.

'*Dios mio,*' he muttered against her lips. '*Te deseo.*' And although Cassandra's grasp of his language was limited at best, she was fairly sure he was saying he wanted her.

Which was madness. Yet, when his tongue probed her lips before plunging deeply into her mouth, she met it with her own, allowing them to mate in a sensuous dance of desire. She was drunk with passion, seduced with longing, lost in the dizzying whirl of the senses.

Enrique's hand cupped the back of her head, angling her mouth to make it easier for him to kiss her. Easier for him to go on delivering those long, drugging kisses that had ignited the flame inside her. He was oblivious of his surroundings, holding her against him with an urgency that suffered no rejection, pressing his hips against hers so that she quickly learned how aroused he was.

She knew her shirt had come free of her trousers when Enrique's hand gripped the bare skin of her midriff. Sliding up beneath the hem of the shirt, his thumb massaged the soft skin beneath her breast. She wound her arms about his neck in mindless surrender. She wished he would touch her breasts; she wanted him to hold them; and for the first time in her life she understood the advantages of not wearing a bra.

She didn't know which of them heard the sound of footsteps first. She thought perhaps that she did. Certainly, she was instantly aware of the sudden chill in the air that had previously been swelteringly hot. But it was Enrique who lifted his head; Enrique whose whole body stiffened in sudden recognition,

Enrique who drew a hoarse breath and somehow managed to regain the initiative by putting her behind him.

'*Mamá!*'

Cassandra understood that word without any difficulty at all. His mother! Her knees felt as if they were about to buckle beneath her. That his mother should find them in such a compromising situation was bad enough. What she would think of her for allowing it to happen didn't bear thinking about.

'Enrique.' The voice that answered him was at best shocked, at worst blatantly hostile. '*Que pasa? Estas loco?*'

Cassandra stiffened. So, his mother thought he was mad, did she? Well, that was scarcely surprising in the circumstances. She must have been mad, too, to let him touch her.

'Speak English, Mamá.' Enrique's response was amazingly cool considering that only moments before he had been making violent love to her. All the same, Cassandra wondered how he was going to explain his actions. In fact, he didn't. 'I did not expect you to arrive so early.'

'Obviously not.' Señora de Montoya's rejoinder was like chipped ice. 'You had far more—pressing matters to attend to, I see.'

'Do not be sarcastic, Mamá. It does not suit you.' Enrique glanced behind him. 'Allow me to introduce you to your daughter-in-law.'

'I think not.'

The contempt in the woman's voice was galling, but Cassandra could hardly blame her. It had been what she was thinking herself, after all. She pulled down her tee shirt and ran smoothing hands over the strands of silky hair escaping from her ponytail. Her swollen mouth would be impossible to disguise, she thought, so perhaps it was just as well.

'You will have to meet her sooner or later,' Enrique was saying calmly, but his mother seemed indifferent to the fact that there was a third person present.

'You expect me to speak to her after this—this fiasco?' she exclaimed incredulously. '*Dios*, Enrique, I cannot believe you are acting this way. After all these years, I am expected to forget what happened to Antonio?' She gave a gasp. 'Never!'

'You are overreacting, Mamá.' Enrique was polite, but inflexible. 'As you say, it is ten years since Antonio's death. Life goes on.'

'And what is that supposed to mean?' His mother was obviously taken aback at this apparent defence of his brother's widow. 'Am I to understand that you are attracted to her? That you are infatuated with her as Antonio was before you? *Dios*, Enrique, I thought you had more sense.'

Now Cassandra had heard enough. She refused to hide behind Enrique as if she was afraid of meeting Antonio's mother. She surely deserved the chance to defend herself. Stepping round her unwanted protector, she confronted the irate little woman across the courtyard.

'Believe me, Señora de Montoya,' she said, annoyed to hear the tremor in her voice, 'I did not choose to be here.' She cast Enrique an accusing look before continuing, 'And nor did I instigate what happened just now. Your son—accosted me as I was looking for David. If you want to blame anyone, blame him.'

Elena de Montoya absorbed this outburst in silence, studying the other woman with critical eyes so that Cassandra was instantly aware of her own shortcomings. In a short-sleeved silk dress in a becoming shade of blue, Elena made up for in presence what she lacked in stature. She was no more than five feet one or two inches tall, but her coronet of sleek black hair and high heels gave her added height. In addition, a double string of what Cassandra guessed were real pearls encircled her throat, and her watch and rings sparkled with jewels. Her appearance would not have disgraced a royal investiture, thought Cassandra wryly, guessing the older woman had dressed this way deliberately. Girded for battle, she reflected, feeling inadequate in her cut-off trousers and cotton top. If only she'd known that Enrique's mother was coming today.

But Elena apparently had no intention of indulging in any verbal sparring with her. 'David?' she said instead, turning back to her son. 'That is the boy's name, is it not? Antonio's son? Where is he?'

'He is watching Juan examine the calves,' replied Enrique

at once, without looking at Cassandra, and she realised with a sense of outrage that his mother was not going to demand any further explanation from him. Whatever she said, whatever she did, Cassandra was the one Elena blamed; Cassandra, who would feel the chill of her displeasure. Cassandra could only hope that David would forgive her if ever the truth of this encounter was exposed.

CHAPTER NINE

'Is THAT agreeable to you, Enrique?'

Miguel de Guzman pointedly cleared his throat after asking the question and Enrique, who had been staring unseeingly through the long windows of the boardroom, turned uncomprehending eyes on the three other men who were gathered at one end of the long polished table.

'I—beg your pardon?'

'I asked if you were willing to allow Viejo to experiment with the vines he brought back from Italy,' explained Miguel patiently. 'Naturally, his experiments would not interfere with current production but, as we all know, without experimentation many of our finer blends would not have been discovered.'

'That is true,' echoed one of his fellow directors, and Enrique inclined his head in acknowledgement.

The famous story of how a wine-maker in the mid-nineteenth century accidentally shipped a barrel of the crystal-clear wine his uncle favoured to England, instead of the dark sweet wine that had been ordered, was the stuff of legend. The wine, subsequently called Tio Pepe, in honour of Manuel Gonzales's uncle, was now one of the top-selling wines in the world, and vintners were constantly experimenting with unique combinations of soil and grape and climate, as well as ageing methods, in the hope of discovering some new favourite.

'I am sure you are right,' Enrique said now, but he had little interest in their concerns today. He had a headache; had had a headache for the past three days, actually. And although he knew he owed it to his father to give his full attention to the business, it was difficult to concentrate when he hadn't had a decent night's sleep since David's letter had arrived.

It had been a stressful week, and ever since his mother's arrival at Tuarega things had gone from bad to worse. The whole household had been left in no doubt as to her feelings and although she had returned to Seville now, Enrique knew it was a temporary reprieve at best.

'Are you all right?'

Miguel de Guzman was looking at him with some concern and Enrique guessed a little of the strain he was feeling must be showing in his face. But, dammit, he had reason to be stressed. His mother had found him kissing the woman he'd sworn he despised more than anyone else on earth.

Yet, when he'd been kissing her, he hadn't despised her. When he'd held her in his arms, when he'd pressed her slim lissom body against his, he'd wanted nothing so much as to—admit it!—bury himself in her soft flesh. He'd wanted, he couldn't deny it, to make love with her, and if his mother hadn't come upon them as she had…

He raked his scalp with agitated fingers. That was what had made his contact with his mother so awkward. Elena de Montoya had been angry at first. He'd known that. But she'd soon recovered and she'd done her best since then to make it easy for him to put the blame elsewhere. She'd wanted him to blame Cassandra. She'd wanted him to say that the woman he had to remember was Antonio's widow had invited his attentions, had encouraged him to take advantage of her so that she could use it against them later.

But he hadn't been able to do it. Which was why he and his mother had failed to have any meaningful conversation while she was here. Cassandra had been foremost in both their minds; Cassandra had stood between them.

Not so with David, however. Although the boy had been somewhat in awe of his Spanish grandmother, he had shown a touching desire to get to know her. Enrique knew that the boy's behaviour left a lot to be desired as far as his mother was concerned: he was far too outspoken for one thing and he didn't behave towards his elders with the respect that Enrique and his brother had had drilled into them from an early age. But although Señora de Montoya had had mixed feelings about the whole situation, she had had to accept that David was her grandson and that her son had had no choice but to tell her about it.

In the end, Enrique had taken the letter to Seville and shown it to his mother. It had seemed the simplest, and possibly the kindest, way to break the news to her. And, although she'd initially expressed doubts about David's parentage, those doubts had ceased, as Enrique's had, as soon as she'd laid eyes on the boy. It was up to her now when, and how, she would tell Enrique's father. Until then, Enrique could only wait and hope that learning he had a grandson would prove a stimulant to Julio's recovery.

Which didn't make his situation any easier, he acknowledged, pulling the file under discussion towards him. It was hard enough to concentrate on everyday things like sleeping and eating at regular times without having to take on the responsibility of making decisions that might affect the future of the estate. All he could think about was that Cassandra was back in his life; Cassandra was at the *palacio*. And that, however eagerly she'd appeared to respond to his lovemaking, her feelings towards him were as hostile as ever.

'I—would prefer we put off taking a vote on this until my father is capable of participating in the discussions,' he said now, aware that he was disappointing them but unable to do anything about it. How could he pass judgement on something so important when he wasn't willing to look beyond the next few days?

The men took his decision resignedly. They weren't prepared to argue with Julio de Montoya's chosen successor, and, with a few polite expressions of goodwill for his father's recovery, they left the boardroom.

Enrique rose at their departure and went to stand at the window. Gazing out at the sweep of the Bay of Cadiz, visible from the elevated heights of the de Montoya building, he massaged the back of his neck with a weary hand. He had handled that well, he thought ironically. Julio would be furious if he knew how ineffectual his contribution had been. His father was depending on him to keep De Montoya y Hijo on course in his absence, but Enrique wondered if he wouldn't have been wiser to appoint Miguel de Guzman as his deputy instead of himself.

He scowled, balling a fist and pressing it against the carved wooden shutters that were folded back against the wall beside the windows. What was wrong with him, for God's sake? Why couldn't he stop thinking about Cassandra and concentrate on the fact that in less than a week his father would be home from the hospital? His mother had said that Julio's doctor was delighted with his progress and that, although he was sixty, Julio apparently had the constitution of a much younger man. It was his father's health that was important, he told himself now, not his own maudlin desire for a woman who had been out of reach as long as he'd known her...

Enrique had been introduced to the woman his brother intended to marry just two weeks before the wedding was due to take place.

He had flown to England on his father's orders to do whatever was necessary to stop the marriage. But, although Julio had told him to warn Antonio that he'd cut him off without a peseta if he went ahead with his plans, Enrique had known that that was a sure-fire way of achieving the exact opposite of what he wanted. Like himself, Antonio had been stubborn, and just quixotic enough to announce that his father could do his worst. And mean it.

In consequence, Enrique had devised a different strategy. He'd had no choice but to admit that his father had sent him, but he'd pretended he was on their side, that he was in favour of the marriage.

It had been pathetically easy to delude Antonio, he remembered, with a pang. His brother had been so open-hearted, so innocent. So sure that what he was doing was right that he hadn't suspected that Enrique might have a different agenda from his own.

In the beginning, Cassandra had been suspicious of him. Perhaps she'd realised even then that he was not to be trusted, though she'd managed to hide her feelings from Antonio.

And, after a few days, even she'd seemed inclined to accept him at face value. After all, he'd been the only member of her future husband's family apparently willing to come to the wedding, and she must have been able to see how delighted Antonio was that he was there.

Antonio had spent much of his time at the university, Enrique remembered. He had been working for his finals. With a degree in art history, he would have had no difficulty in getting a job with or without his father's approval, but it had meant that Enrique and Cassandra had spent a lot of time alone together. Her job at the local library had been much more flexible, and Antonio had insisted that she should get to know his brother.

Looking back now, Enrique knew a reluctance to re-examine his feelings at that time. When had he determined that the only way to stop the marriage had been to seduce her himself? When had he finally decided that his brother was making a mistake and it was up to him to prove it?

God, how arrogant he had been! Of course, he'd been convinced that she was only marrying Antonio because of what she expected to get out of it. Antonio's declaration that it had been love at first sight had sounded far too convenient, and he'd been sure that if Cassandra thought *he* was attracted to her, too, she'd instantly see the advantages of marrying the elder son. He was his father's heir, after all. Not Antonio.

He blew out a breath. Had he really thought it would be that simple? All right, he had only been twenty-four, and life had still been painted in colours of black and white, but he found it hard now to credit his belief in his own infallibility.

Nevertheless, he had sensed that Cassandra was aware of him. No matter how she'd tried to hide it, he'd seen the way she'd looked at him, the way she'd listened intently to everything he'd said. She'd thought she was just being friendly, but Enrique had recognised the signs. Unfortunately, she hadn't until it was much too late to save herself.

And he hadn't been totally indifferent to her, he remembered grimly. She had been—she was—a beautiful woman, and, with short skirts and bare legs, she had been much different from the constrained Catholic girls he'd known back home. In Spain, even today, young women of good families did not go about so freely. They were guarded and protected until they had a ring on their finger.

Perhaps that was what had attracted Antonio to her, too, although his brother had always been drawn to tall slim women with long legs and high breasts. Even without the curly mass of red-gold hair that tumbled about her shoulders, she'd been stunning, and Enrique had to concede that he wouldn't have been human if he hadn't found her stunning as well.

But it wasn't just her looks that had appealed to him, he acknowledged. In the days they had spent together, it had been her warmth and her personality that had made the task he had set himself so enjoyable. But also so difficult. She had shown him parts of London he hadn't known existed, sharing her knowledge generously, making him laugh with the many anecdotes she could recite about the famous people who had once lived in the city.

Perhaps that was when she'd started to lower her guard with him, Enrique reflected. She'd still been wary of him, of course, still unconvinced, perhaps, that both brothers would be prepared to defy their father in such a way. She'd known that Julio de Montoya was not in favour of their marriage, and that had made her cautious of trusting his deputy. But, gradually, Enrique had gained her confidence, and, despite himself, he'd been drawn to her unaffected charm.

So much so that he'd begun to resent the evenings when his brother had joined them, remembered Enrique bitterly. He wasn't proud of it, but he'd resented his brother touching her in ways he himself had wanted to touch her. And when Antonio had put his arms around her, and kissed her, Enrique had felt emotions he didn't even want to identify today…

Cassandra was sitting in the shade of the balcony outside their apartments when David came to find her.

She hadn't seen her son since early that morning. Now that his grandmother had gone back to Seville, he'd taken the first opportunity to go and find Juan Martinez. And, although

Cassandra was always anxious when he was out with the stockman, she'd accepted Carlos Mendoza's word that no harm would come to him at the *palacio*.

'He is *el patrón's* heir,' he'd said simply, and Cassandra had wondered if he knew how true that was.

But of course he didn't. None of them did. David was Antonio's son; Julio de Montoya's grandson. That was enough.

She and Carlos had struck up an unlikely friendship. Enrique's major-domo had done his best to make her feel at home at the *palacio*, and it was he who had taken her to the small chapel in the grounds and shown her where her husband was buried. Antonio had joined his ancestors in the stone *sepulcro* that bore his family's name, and Cassandra had stood for several minutes, feeling the peace that enveloped the place stealing about her.

Elena de Montoya was a different matter, however. Yet, despite her outrage at finding her son kissing his brother's widow, she, too, had recognised at once that David was a de Montoya. And although, to Cassandra's knowledge, she hadn't shown any affection towards him, she had spent several hours talking with him, learning about him, about his life in England, resenting her daughter-in-law's presence at these interviews, resenting her for keeping his existence a secret for so long.

Not that Cassandra cared what Enrique's mother thought of her. Elena de Montoya hadn't wanted to know her ten years ago and there was no doubt she'd prefer not to have to acknowledge her now. But, in that respect, David's attitude had been pivotal, and the older woman had been forced to behave at least politely towards her daughter-in-law when her grandson was present. They'd maintained a stiff formality that was as cold as it was artificial, but thankfully David had been too overawed at meeting his grandmother at last to notice.

Yet, she appended uneasily. Sooner or later, he was going to recognise the hostility for what it was, and then what excuse would she make? Cassandra didn't want to think about that now. She had too many other problems to contend with. Not least, Enrique...

Not that she'd spent any time alone with him since the morning of his mother's arrival. The memory of the scene Elena de Montoya had interrupted was too painful to consider objectively, and since then she'd done everything she could to keep out of his way. Fortunately, David wasn't expected to join the family for dinner because of his age, and, consciously or unconsciously on their part, it had given her the perfect excuse to stay with her son.

Of course, that hadn't prevented her from thinking about Enrique, and about what might have happened if his mother hadn't interrupted them. My God, she thought incredulously, she'd thought she was immune from any sexual attraction to him. Despite her awareness of Enrique, she'd really believed that nothing he did could make her lose control.

How wrong she'd been. As soon as he'd touched her, as soon as he'd fastened his lips to hers, she'd been like putty in his hands. And when he'd thrust his tongue into her mouth she'd been helpless. She'd had no defence against the raw emotion that had torn her defences aside.

Now, as she looked at her son, she had to acknowledge that, even in the few days that they'd been here, David had changed. She didn't know how exactly. She wouldn't have thought anything his grandmother had said to him could have caused the breach. He was more tanned than he'd been when they left Punta del Lobo, and he'd stopped putting the gel on his hair that had proved such a bone of contention before they'd left England. Now, his hair gleamed glossy and black in the sunlight, as thick and lustrous, though perhaps not as long, as Enrique's. But the change wasn't just physical. David seemed more confident; more respectful; older, even. He was beginning to behave as if he belonged here, she realised with sudden apprehension. As if Tuarega, and not the small semi in Hemmingway Close, was his home.

The realisation made her irritable, and her voice was that much sharper than it should have been when she said, 'Where have you been? It's almost two o'clock! Have you had lunch? Did you wear a hat as I told you?'

David's mouth compressed. 'I don't need a hat, Mum,' he

exclaimed, answering her last question first. 'Uncle Enrique doesn't wear a hat. Why should I?'

Cassandra's lips tightened. How tired she was of hearing Enrique quoted at every turn. David had shown no particular desire to spend more time with his grandmother, but Enrique was different. He obviously had great respect for his uncle, however much he might initially have resented him for disciplining him when he'd run away.

But then, that was hardly surprising, Cassandra conceded. Enrique was exactly the kind of dominant male her son would admire. Her own father had inspired affection, but David had always been able to run rings around him. Enrique was different. Dear Lord, did she need any more proof than she had already?

'Your—uncle doesn't need a hat because he was born here,' she told her son now, her voice clipped and impatient. 'He's used to this climate, David. You're not.'

'I'll get used to it,' said David carelessly, lifting his thin shoulders in a dismissive shrug. 'Where is Uncle Enrique anyway? I thought he'd be back from Cadiz by now.'

'He may well be,' said Cassandra, closing the book which had been lying open and unread on her lap. 'You're not his keeper, David. Enrique comes and goes as he pleases. You should know that.'

David sighed. 'What's wrong, Mum?' he exclaimed, not without justification. 'Why are you so crabby? I only asked where Uncle Enrique was. I wanted to tell him what I'd been doing today.'

Cassandra stiffened. 'What have you been doing?'

'Are you really interested?' David left her side to saunter across to the pool, dipping his hands into the cool water and splashing it over his wrists. 'All you ever do is spoil things. I know you didn't want to come here, but I don't see why you can't enjoy it anyway.'

Cassandra caught her breath. 'I—I don't spoil things,' she protested, aware of a slight tremor in her voice. 'David, that's an awful thing to say. And totally unfair. I was worried about you, that's all. You're just a child. You may enjoy watching the animals, but you shouldn't forget that they're dangerous.'

'Horses aren't dangerous,' retorted David, swinging round to face her. 'That was what I wanted to tell Uncle Enrique. Juan has found me a horse of my own. I've been riding round the paddock all morning.'

'A horse?' Cassandra didn't know whether to be relieved or dismayed. 'Do you mean a pony? Boys of your age don't ride horses, do they?'

'Uncle Enrique did,' said David, and Cassandra wanted to scream that *Uncle Enrique* was no role model for him to imitate.

'Anyway, Duquesa is a mare,' he went on, evidently proud of his achievement. 'She's not as big as Santa Cruz, that's Uncle Enrique's horse, but Juan says she's not a *caballito* either.'

'What is a *caballito*?' asked Cassandra, frowning, and then saw her son's face brighten with delight. But he was looking over her shoulder, not at her, and she was hardly surprised when Enrique answered her.

'It means a hobbyhorse,' he said, crossing into her line of vision. 'I told Juan to find a mount for David. If he has chosen Duquesa, he has chosen well.'

Cassandra looked up at him with hostile eyes. He was standing with his back to the sunlight, which meant his dark face was unreadable from this angle. But in a light grey suit that complemented his powerful frame, the jacket hooked lazily over one shoulder, he was still impressive. Impressive and disturbing, she thought uneasily, aware that even the air had quickened since he had stepped into the courtyard.

'I don't remember anyone asking me if David should be allowed to ride,' she said a little jealously, getting up from the low cushioned lounger where she had been sitting, and shading her eyes with a slightly unsteady hand.

'Oh, Mum!' Once again, David showed his impatience at her negativity. 'Why shouldn't I learn to ride? Everyone rides around here.'

'I don't,' retorted Cassandra at once, and saw Enrique's eyes take on a sardonic glint.

'That can be arranged,' he said smoothly, completely out-witting her defence. 'I myself will teach you. You will enjoy it. It will enable you to go freely about the estate. Is tomorrow too soon for your first lesson?'

Cassandra drew a breath. 'I don't wish to learn to ride, thank you,' she said, earning another exasperated sigh from her son. 'I just meant I would have liked to have been consulted about David's activities. He is still my son, however much you might wish it wasn't so.'

'What are you talking about, Mum?' Too late, Cassandra realised she had spoken rather rashly. 'Why should Uncle Enrique wish you weren't my mother? You were his brother's wife.'

'Your mother is a little annoyed with me, that is all, David,' inserted Enrique swiftly. 'I think perhaps it would be a good idea if you went to your room for a rest. You must be tired. Riding can be very exhausting. Besides, I wish to speak to your mother alone.'

'Oh, but—'

David was about to object when he thought better of it. And Cassandra, who resented the idea that Enrique could control her son far more easily than she could, quickly endorsed his words. 'Yes, do that, David,' she said, as if her contribution was the deciding factor. 'We'll continue our discussion later.'

David looked less happy at this interjection, but Cassandra couldn't help that. She had no real desire to be left alone with Enrique, but David had to learn that she was not abrogating her responsibility for him just because he considered his un-cle's orders carried more weight. She was his mother. Her opinion mattered.

Nevertheless, she was incredibly tense. And, when David disappeared into the building behind them, she was uneasily aware of Enrique watching her with dark brooding eyes. But what was most disturbing was the realisation that he'd had no compunction about invading her part of the *palacio*. She had thought she was safe here. How wrong she had been!

'Stop looking at me as if you do not trust me,' he said abruptly, flinging his jacket onto the chair beside her. 'I know you have been avoiding me, but it is not necessary.'

'Isn't it?' Cassandra couldn't stand still under his abrasive scrutiny. 'Has your mother warned you not to overstep the mark again?' she asked sarcastically, stepping out into the sunlight. 'It's good to know that someone has some control over you.'

Enrique's eyes flashed with sudden anger. 'My mother knows better than to try and tell me what to do,' he retorted harshly. And then, as if realising she was deliberately provoking him, he added, 'In any case, there was no need for her to say anything. What happened between us was a mistake. It will not happen again.'

Cassandra absorbed these words with a mixture of relief and resentment. He was so arrogant, she thought. So sure of himself. It would be almost worth the pain it would no doubt cause her to prove to him that he wasn't half as in control as he believed.

But that way lay madness, particularly as she already knew he was involved with another woman. So, putting all thoughts of pursuing that aside, she said, 'So what did you want to talk to me about? Has your mother told you to get me out of here before your father comes home?'

Enrique swore softly. 'Will you stop implying that I am answerable to anyone but myself?' he demanded. 'It may interest you to know that for the past eighteen months I have been in virtual control of both the estate and the winery. That is why I am living in the *palacio* again instead of at my own house.'

Cassandra's eyes widened. 'You have your own house?'

'Is that so surprising? I am thirty-four, Cassandra. I lead my own life.'

'And—your house: is it far from here?'

'Why do you want to know?' Now it was his turn to be sardonic. 'Would you like to see it?'

Cassandra lifted her shoulders in an eloquent gesture. 'Of course not. But your work is here. I'd have thought—'

'It is on the estate,' put in Enrique drily. 'My house is on the estate. Further up the valley. A much more modest dwelling than this, but I like it.'

Cassandra couldn't prevent herself. 'You surprise me,' she said drily. 'I'd have thought Tuarega was much more to your taste.'

'Which just goes to show how little you know me,' he retorted, his eyes dropping with sudden concern to her unprotected shoulders. 'Your arms are getting burned. We should continue this discussion indoors.'

Oh, no! Cassandra moved instinctively away from him, deliberately putting more space between them. She had no intention of inviting him into her living room. Although he'd violated the neutrality of her courtyard, she could still pretend that their apartments were their own.

'I'm all right,' she said, brushing a careless hand over her hot skin. 'Why don't you tell me what you want and then I can get on with what I was doing?'

'Cassandra!' His voice was curiously rough as he followed her across to the pool. 'When are you going to stop fighting me?'

Cassandra shook her head. 'You said yourself that any contact between us was a mistake. Why should it matter to you what I think of you?'

'I do not know.' There was harshness in his tone now. Then, with obvious unwillingness, 'But it does.'

Cassandra's eyes were drawn to him then. His reply had been so unexpected, and although she'd toyed with the thought of baiting him earlier, she hadn't really expected this response.

'I don't think you mean that,' she said at last, her voice not altogether steady. 'Please: I'm sure you've got better things to do than waste my time and yours.'

Enrique's lips twisted. 'You enjoy insulting me, do you not?'

'I just want you to go,' exclaimed Cassandra, driven beyond endurance. 'I'm sure your mother wouldn't approve of this conversation.'

Enrique frowned. 'My mother is not my keeper,' he said,

the intensity of his gaze increasing as he absorbed her words. 'And I did not come here to speak about family matters, as it happens.'

'No?' Cassandra's nails dug into her palms. 'Then what? The woman you deny is your girlfriend, perhaps?'

Enrique pulled his tie away from his collar, exposing the brown column of his throat to her unwilling gaze. 'You persist in provoking me, Cassandra,' he said wryly. 'But, as it happens, I am glad you brought her name up. Sanchia, the woman I explained that Antonio was betrothed to, is coming here this evening. I think it would be a good idea if you joined us for dinner.'

CHAPTER TEN

WHY had she agreed to such a crazy scheme?

As Cassandra prepared for dinner that evening, she berated herself again for agreeing to Enrique's request. She could have refused. She could have ignored his invitation and not laid herself open to possible insult and injury. But curiosity had got the better of her and she was ashamed to say that she wanted to see the woman that both Antonio and Enrique had loved.

Yet, if she was totally honest with herself, she had to admit that that wasn't the only reason. Antonio had told her about Sanchia de Silvestre. He'd said how he suspected she'd really wanted to marry Enrique and, when he'd shown that he wasn't interested, she'd transferred her attentions to his younger brother. Now, it seemed, she was getting her wish, and Cassandra couldn't deny that she was curious to see her and Enrique together.

And how intelligent was that?

Peering at her reflection in the long carved mirror in her bedroom, Cassandra couldn't avoid the sudden anguish in her eyes. She had thought, she'd really *believed*, that nothing Enrique did could hurt her any more. But it wasn't true. He'd always had the power to reduce her defences to ashes and she just kept on letting him do it...

When had she first realised that she was attracted to Enrique? How long before she'd begun to look forward to the time they spent together? Why had she fooled herself that her feelings for Enrique were innocent of any sexual intent?

Because she hadn't wanted to admit it, she acknowledged now. All those days they'd spent together when Antonio was finishing his exams: she'd let Enrique get close, so close, never

109

suspecting that his agenda had been so cruelly different from her own.

Looking back, it was easy to be wise after the event. Easy to tell herself that she should have known that a man like Enrique de Montoya, a man with his background, his prospects, was unlikely to be seriously attracted to a penniless librarian. Yet he'd been so likeable, so charming, so unconsciously sexy that, before she'd known it, she'd been totally fascinated.

Totally *infatuated*, she amended bitterly, remembering with a shameful pang how helpless she'd been against his sensual assault.

But it had begun innocently enough, she remembered. So innocently that she hadn't known what was happening until it was much too late to do anything about it.

Ten years ago, she'd been living in a bedsit just off the Edgware Road. Although her widowed father lived just a few miles away in the suburbs, she'd decided to get her own place when she'd got the job at the Kensington Historical Library. She'd wanted to be independent; she'd wanted to live her own life.

And it was through the library that she'd met Antonio. He'd come into her department to do some research, and until his brother came on the scene she'd never had any doubts that she loved him.

Of course, Antonio hadn't told her he was engaged to a young woman back home in Andalucia. He'd let her think he was as unattached and fancy-free as she was herself. It hadn't been until they'd started talking about getting married that he'd confessed that he hadn't told her the complete truth.

At first, she'd wanted to call the whole thing off. But Antonio had persuaded her that, whatever happened between them, his engagement to the Spanish girl was over. He loved her and if she wouldn't marry him he'd spend the rest of his life alone.

Overly dramatic, perhaps, Cassandra thought now, but she'd wanted to believe him. He'd even shown her the letter he'd written to Sanchia and she'd eventually given in, and they'd arranged to get married as soon as his final exams were over.

She knew he'd doubted that any of his family would turn up for the wedding. He'd written to his father, too, telling him that he was in love with an English girl, but Julio de Montoya hadn't replied. Instead, he'd sent his elder son to accomplish what he'd known his words alone would not achieve, and Cassandra had been thrown into contact with the man who was to have such a fateful influence on her life.

Yet, to begin with, it hadn't seemed that way. Although she herself had been a little anxious when Enrique appeared, Antonio had been so delighted to see him she'd soon buried her own doubts and accepted his presence at face value.

And it hadn't been difficult. Enrique was sufficiently like Antonio to make their rapport with one another seem not only easy but natural, and when he had started showing his attraction for her she had persuaded herself that he was just being kind.

Taking her hand when they were crossing a busy road; a light pressure in the small of her back when he was guiding her into a bar or a restaurant; a careless stroke on her neck; his thigh brushing hers when they shared a sofa or a banquette. These were the things he'd used to make her aware of him, and she, idiot that she was, had been completely overwhelmed by it all. Why hadn't she realised what he was doing? she wondered. Why had she trusted him?

The truth was that she'd been flattered. Flattered that he was paying her so much attention; flattered that he seemed to enjoy being with her. She'd enjoyed being with him, and if she'd sometimes indulged in daydreams about what it would be like to make love with Enrique, she'd excused herself on the grounds that because she was still a virgin she was naturally curious about sex.

Curious!

Cassandra shivered. God, that was such an inadequate word to describe how she'd felt about Enrique. She'd been aware of him with every fibre of her being, and when they were together she'd found it incredibly difficult to think about anyone else. She supposed she'd wanted him—although she hadn't known then what wanting meant.

She decided that that must have been when she'd started noticing the differences between the brothers. Both men had been tall and dark, but Enrique was taller, darker, with a sexual magnetism that Cassandra had begun to find increasingly hard to ignore. What she'd found attractive about Antonio had been accentuated in Enrique, like finding the original of a painting after getting used to a copy. A very appealing copy, she acknowledged wryly, but a copy nonetheless.

A couple of days before the wedding, she and Antonio had arranged to go down to Essex to visit her father. He and her sisters were coming to the ceremony, of course, but Cassandra had wanted to see them, to finalise the details for the following weekend. Perhaps she'd unconsciously been searching for confirmation of her decision, Cassandra reflected now. Her sisters had been so enthusiastic. It had been easier with them to convince herself that she was doing the right thing.

But, at the last minute, Antonio had asked if she'd mind if he didn't accompany her. There was to be a reception for graduating foreign students that evening, he'd explained apologetically, but he'd spoken to Enrique and his brother was more than happy to take his place.

How cruelly right he'd been, thought Cassandra bitterly. And, although she'd insisted she was quite capable of going alone—and had done so—Enrique had been waiting for her when she'd got back to St Pancras Station.

'Railways stations are not the place for single women,' he'd declared, when she'd questioned his presence, and although she'd argued the point she couldn't deny she'd been touched that he should have spent the better part of an hour waiting for her.

They'd taken a taxi to her lodgings and it had seemed only polite to invite him in for a coffee. It was the first time any man but Antonio had entered her bedsit, and almost at once she'd realised her mistake. Enrique's dark masculinity had dominated the modest contours of her room and although she had never felt intimidated by Antonio's presence, Enrique was a whole different ball game.

While she'd added coffee to the filter one of her sisters had bought her as a housewarming present, Enrique had wandered about the room, picking up a picture here, adjusting an ornament there. She'd wished he would sit down, but apart from the two dining chairs that had flanked her folding table there'd been only the divan she'd slept on. And although she'd added a coloured throw for daytime use, it had still been far too personal for her peace of mind.

Eventually he had subsided onto the divan, sitting on the edge, his legs spread wide, his lean wrists hanging between. He'd looked so attractive sitting there, his head bent to expose the unexpectedly vulnerable curve of his nape. She'd found herself wanting to touch his neck, to slide her hand into the darkness of his hair, to feel the thick lustrous strands curling about her fingers. But, of course, she hadn't touched him. Not then. She'd realised—or at least she'd *believed*—that he was as nervous about the situation as she was. And that had made what had happened afterwards so infinitely hard to forgive.

At the time, however, she'd been perfectly willing to accept his behaviour at face value, and when the coffee was ready, she'd carried both cups to the divan and seated herself beside him. He'd been wearing a leather jerkin, she remembered. Black, like the close-fitting jeans he'd worn with it, his dark blue shirt the only trace of colour in his outfit. He'd always worn his clothes well; both men had. But whereas Antonio had merely looked good, Enrique's outfit had moulded his powerful body with loving elegance.

'This is good,' he'd said, indicating the coffee, and Cassandra remembered feeling pleased at the compliment. So pleased that she'd offered to get him a second cup. But, when she'd put down her cup and attempted to get to her feet, Enrique had caught her wrist, drawing her back down beside him. 'Later,' he'd told her huskily, and when she'd looked into his eyes, she'd known exactly what he meant.

She should have stopped him. She should have covered her lips with her hand and prevented his from finding their target.

But she hadn't. She'd lifted her hands, yes, but instead of blocking his searching mouth she'd cupped his neck and given herself up to the union they'd both desired.

Or she'd thought it was what they'd both desired, she amended bitterly. At the time, she'd been too blinded by her own needs to notice his response. It had been enough that he was kissing her at last, that his weight was compelling her back against the cushions behind her. That his hard muscled body was aroused and urgent; that his kiss was full of emotion.

But what those emotions might have portrayed, she hadn't questioned. Why should she have? She'd been so sure that Enrique felt the way she did, and although she'd felt guilty for betraying Antonio, she'd assured herself naïvely that he would understand. Once he realised that she and Enrique loved one another—

How deluded she'd been! How stupid! How pathetic!

Remembering now, Cassandra was appalled anew at her own gullibility. She'd really believed that Enrique cared about her, that he'd been as helpless in the face of such powerful feelings as she'd been.

What a fool!

Nevertheless, however calculated his approach, she was sure he'd been shocked by the passion that had erupted between them. However cynically he'd set out on his plan to discredit her, what had happened had driven all thoughts of revenge out of his head. For a time, anyway. He'd wanted her just as much as she'd wanted him, and perhaps it was that knowledge that had made what had happened so much more significant, so much more devastating.

To begin with she'd thought he'd only meant to kiss her. She'd been innocent, trusting, so used to Antonio, who had always respected her wish to remain a virgin until they were married, that the idea of Enrique abusing that trust hadn't occurred to her.

She should have known better. Now, she realised, she should have known at once that Enrique was nothing like Antonio. The way he'd kissed her, the way he'd crushed her lips, the sensual way he'd pushed his tongue into her mouth;

so many things should have warned her that she was playing with fire.

Perhaps they had. If she was completely honest she would have to admit that she'd never been in any doubt who was making love to her. Enrique had been so much more eager; so much more demanding; so much more *experienced*. Yes, that was the word to describe Enrique's lovemaking: experienced. He'd known exactly what he'd wanted, and he'd had no intention of allowing anything to stand in his way.

Least of all a foolish girl to whom his practised caresses had seemed a natural forerunner to romance. She'd convinced herself that Enrique had fallen in love with her and, although that was no excuse for what had happened, it had been enough to salve her conscience at the time.

And, with Enrique's weight imprisoning her beneath him on the divan, she'd been left in little doubt as to his body's reaction to what they were doing. His breathing had been as ragged as hers, laboured gulps of air snatched between long, soul-drugging kisses, that had stifled any protest and left her weak with longing. The throbbing heat of his arousal had pressed against her stomach, and need, hot and unfamiliar, had poured through her.

Neither before nor since had she felt such powerful emotions. She'd been lost to all sanity, lost to all shame. It had felt so good, so right, and there'd been no way she could have prevented what had happened, however humiliated it made her feel now.

She remembered pushing Enrique's jacket off his shoulders, sliding her hands into the open neck of his shirt, touching the warm flesh at his nape which had inspired such forbidden feelings in her earlier. The moist hair had curled about her fingers and she'd used it to drag his sensual mouth back to hers.

Enrique's hands had found the buttons on her shirt, she recalled, her breathing quickening in remembrance. The tiny pearl studs had been no match for his searching fingers, and her breasts had become hot and heavy beneath the lacy confinement of her bra. She'd wanted him to touch them. She'd actually ached with the need for him to do so. So much so that she'd managed to arch her body so that she could release the catch of her bra herself.

God, she'd been so easy, she fretted unsteadily. So desperate for him not to stop what he was doing that she'd have stripped herself naked if he'd asked her to. But he hadn't. He'd been quite content to attend to that detail himself. Nevertheless, he must have thought she knew what she was doing, she conceded unwillingly. She hadn't behaved as if it had been her first time, that was a fact.

He'd shed his own shirt a few moments later, letting her help him peel the fine fabric from his bronzed skin. His chest had been lightly spread with dark hair, she recollected with a shiver. A sensual covering that had arrowed down into the waistband of his trousers.

Her own skirt had been discarded next, and she remembered the disturbing brush of his chest hair against her bare stomach when he lowered himself to take her breast into his mouth. The sensation of his tongue circling her nipple, sucking on the tender tip, had left her breathless, and her breasts tingled now in protest at the direction of her thoughts.

She remembered unbuckling his belt, drawing down his zip, touching him between his legs with tentative fingers. He'd shuddered at her timid caress, but he hadn't objected, rolling to one side to divest himself of both his trousers and his shorts.

It wasn't until his hands had slid beneath her bottom, drawing her up against him, that she'd experienced any trepidation about what they were doing. When the pulsating heat of his maleness had probed the moist triangle of curls at the apex of her legs, she'd known an instant's sheer panic. She ought to tell him, she'd thought anxiously. She ought to warn him that she was a virgin. But she'd been afraid that if he'd known the truth he might have drawn away.

In any case, that was the last coherent thought she'd had. Enrique's fingers had found the sensitive cleft of her bottom, sliding between to explore the pulsing entrance to her womanhood. She'd been wet. She'd felt it on his hands, she recalled tensely. Her untried senses had swum with her first taste of her own sexuality.

She'd been aroused and eager, she remembered now, so that Enrique had never suspected he'd have any problem achieving his own ends. As it happened, he hadn't become aware of her innocence until he'd thrust into her, and by then it had been much too late. He was inside her, filling her, expanding her tight muscles with his powerful shaft. Cursing her perhaps, she thought now, but needing her, creating a mindless excitement that only complete surrender on both their parts could have assuaged.

And had, she recalled, but without bitterness for once. She supposed she ought to be grateful. Many a woman's first experience of sex was with a vastly inferior partner, whereas Enrique, whatever his private agenda, had made sure she'd stayed with him all the way. She'd spun out into infinite space only seconds before he'd achieved his own climax, when the flooding heat of him spilling into her had reminded her that she hadn't thought of the consequences that might ensue…

Shaking her head now, Cassandra reached for her hairbrush, using it on her newly washed hair with unwarranted violence. But remembering what had happened did that to her. It left her feeling weak and vulnerable even after all this time.

The idea that she might be pregnant hadn't become a reality until much later. At that time, she'd still believed that she and Enrique had a future together. She'd believed they were a couple; that they would tell Antonio the following day that they loved one another. Then, whatever happened, Enrique would stand by her.

Another big mistake.

Despite having taken her innocence, despite the fact that he must have known when he'd left that she'd expected to see him the next morning, he'd told her nothing of his plans. When he'd departed in the early hours, going silently down the stairs so as not to alert Cassandra's landlady, he'd kissed her goodbye with a lingering passion that she'd been convinced was genuine. She'd gone back to bed and spent the rest of the night dreaming about him, never imagining that, as far as Enrique was concerned, he'd achieved his objective. He'd had no intention of ever seeing her again.

Of course, when she'd awakened the next day, she'd faced the prospect of telling Antonio what had happened with some trepidation. And regret. She had loved Antonio. She had cared about him. But compared to the way she'd felt about Enrique, the feelings she'd had for her fiancé just didn't compete.

Learning from Antonio later that morning that Enrique had left to return to Spain had been a shock, but her fiancé had had even worse news to relate. Although Enrique had obviously not told his brother that he'd seduced his fiancée, he had admitted that he'd had reservations about Cassandra's suitability all along. He'd maintained that he couldn't, in all conscience, attend a wedding that he and his father opposed, and his advice had been that Antonio should think again before incurring their father's wrath over a woman who wasn't worthy to bear the de Montoya name.

Cassandra had been stunned. There had been no way she could convince herself that this was Enrique's way of preventing the wedding. Whatever he was—and she'd eventually come to regard him as a monster—she hadn't believed he was a coward. If he'd cared anything for her, he'd have stayed and faced his brother like a man.

She'd eventually had to accept that what had happened between them had been a carefully orchestrated seduction. However emotionally involved he'd seemed, for him she had been just another woman, another body in which to slake his lust. He hadn't loved her. She doubted he could love anyone besides himself. He'd tricked her and he'd used her, and she'd been left to pay the price.

Even so, she'd known that she couldn't marry Antonio now. However despicable Enrique's behaviour had been, it had proved to her that her feelings for her fiancé were not strong enough to stand the test of time. But when she'd tried to convey this to Antonio, he'd refused to listen to her. As far as he'd been concerned, she was only responding to his brother's censure, and he'd begged her not to shame him now and confirm his family's judgement about her.

It seemed that Enrique hadn't confessed his own betrayal. And how could she have told Antonio what Enrique had done? She'd loved him too much to hurt him so badly. He would have been permanently damaged; totally devastated. Whatever her faults, she hadn't been that cruel.

So she had allowed the marriage to go ahead, telling herself that the hatred she had now conceived for Enrique had no part in it. She had loved Antonio, after all. She'd determined to make him a good wife. But she'd been nineteen, and, as Enrique had discovered, totally inexperienced. It was only now she realised that she'd been in a state of shock. She'd been in no way capable of making any rational decisions about her future at that time.

The wedding had gone ahead as planned, and Antonio had been content. He'd been disappointed by his brother's absence, of course. But one of Cassandra's brothers-in-law had stepped in as best man in Enrique's place. The marriage at the local register office had served its purpose. Cassandra's father and sisters had been there to support her, and if they'd thought the bride looked to be in something of a daze, they'd said nothing to mar the event.

It had been raining when they'd left to drive down to Cornwall, she remembered. The roads had been slick and wet and Antonio had been driving an unfamiliar car. It was one he had hired for their honeymoon and he had not been an experienced driver. But, even so, it hadn't been his fault when the huge articulated vehicle ahead of them jack-knifed on the slippery tarmac.

The rear end of the wagon had hit the nearside wing of their car, crushing the steering wheel against the window, so that the airbag, which had inflated, had offered Antonio no protection at all. He'd been killed instantly, and Cassandra, who'd suffered only minor injuries, had regained consciousness in the ambulance. And, when she'd asked about her husband, they'd told her regretfully, but unalterably, that she was a widow.

Expelling an unsteady breath, Cassandra put down the hairbrush now and stared bleakly at her reflection. Antonio's family had been quick enough to come to his funeral, she recalled painfully, despising the fact that it still hurt her to think of it. His mother hadn't attended, but Julio de Montoya and his elder son had been there. Not that either of them had spoken to her, she acknowledged bitterly. Even though she'd agreed, via the Spanish lawyer who had contacted her, to allow Antonio's body to be removed to Spain for burial, she had received no thanks from them. She hadn't even known where he was buried, until Carlos had shown her. When David was born— Enrique's son, of course—she'd told him that his father had died in a car crash just after they were married, and thankfully her son had never questioned why they'd never visited his father's grave.

CHAPTER ELEVEN

ENRIQUE raised his wine glass to his lips, watching with dark hooded eyes as Cassandra responded to something Luis Banderas had said. The Spaniard, a distant cousin whom he'd invited to even the numbers at dinner, was evidently fascinated by the fair-skinned Englishwoman. He'd had eyes for no one else since she appeared and Enrique, who had foolishly imagined that Luis would remove the need for him to spend the whole evening entertaining Sanchia, was left in the unenviable position of having to be nice to the woman for whom he had suddenly acquired a distinct aversion.

Meanwhile, Luis was enjoying himself immensely. The meal was over and for the past fifteen minutes he'd been describing the religious festival that took place on his family's estate when the grapes were harvested. Although Enrique felt sure Cassandra couldn't be that interested, she was gazing at Luis as if every word he spoke was of the utmost importance to her, and it infuriated him.

Enrique's jaw compressed. He knew what she was doing, he thought. As far as she was concerned, Luis was the first person she'd met since she came here who had treated her with any kind of respect. His mother had insulted her, and Sanchia, although she'd been polite, had made no attempt to hide the contempt in her eyes.

But what had he expected? Enrique asked himself impatiently. In Sanchia's eyes, Cassandra was an intruder; an interloper. The woman who had stolen her fiancé and who now had the audacity to come here, bringing an heir to the de Montoya estate with her.

He dragged his eyes away from Cassandra's expressive features and stared down, grim-faced, into the wine in his glass. Thinking about David wasn't conducive to his mood either.

In recent days, as he'd recovered from the shock of learning he had a nephew, he'd discovered that his feelings towards the boy were no less ambivalent. As his unwilling awareness of Cassandra had deepened, he'd found himself disliking the fact that David was Antonio's son and not his. He should have been his son, he brooded, and then was ashamed of the thought. But he had to concede that he resented the idea that Cassandra had turned instantly to Antonio for comfort as soon as he'd deserted her.

Or had she?

His head jerked up and he stared intently at her lightly flushed profile. The sun had already laid its fingers on her and the touch of colour suited her, but Enrique noticed these things without really being conscious of them. His mind was full of the question he had just posed himself, and, while it might sound very intriguing to probe the hypothesis, did he really want to know?

'What are you thinking about, *querido*?' Sanchia spoke softly in Spanish, stretching out her hand to cover his where it lay beside his glass. 'I cannot believe you are enjoying this—this evening any more than I am.'

'You are wrong.' Enrique spoke in English, aware that his words must have been clearly audible to the other couple at the table. His eyes challenged the Spanish woman's. 'But if you are bored…'

Sanchia's lips tightened and for a moment he thought she had taken umbrage at his insensitivity. He half hoped she had. But, with an obvious effort, she gathered herself and regarded him with seductive eyes. 'How could I be bored when I am with you, *querido*?' she asked, using English as he had done, but, judging by the way she included Cassandra in her sweeping gaze, for different reasons. She squeezed his hand. 'Is there any chance of us spending the rest of the evening alone?'

Enrique withdrew his hand with careful deliberation. 'Would you have me neglect my other guests?' he asked smoothly, picking up the wine bottle and offering to refill her glass. 'Shall we have another bottle of this? It is rather good.'

Sanchia covered her glass with her hand, and almost instinctually Enrique was aware that Cassandra's head had turned in their direction. What had she thought Sanchia had been saying when she'd spoken in their own language? he wondered irritably. Certainly not what had been said, judging by what had come after. Did she think he and Sanchia were conducting a flirtation at the table? The idea was distasteful to him.

'Wine?' he asked, his eyes holding Cassandra's even when he knew she wanted to look away, but she shook her head.

'Not for me, thank you,' she said, the two long strands of silky-soft hair that she'd left to curl in front of her ears shining red-gold in the candlelight. She'd wound the rest of her hair into a precariously secured knot on the top of her head this evening and Enrique had to stifle an almost uncontrollable impulse to tear out the pins and bury his face in its vivid beauty.

Whether Cassandra had sensed what he was thinking, he didn't know, but something gave her the will to break that revealing eye contact. And Luis's cheerful intervention at that moment was clearly a relief to her.

'*Por favor*, Enrique,' he said, pushing his glass towards the other man. Then, to his companion, 'My cousin keeps an excellent cellar, do you not think so?'

'I don't know very much about wine,' answered Cassandra honestly. 'I didn't even know that Rioja could be white as well as red until I came here.'

'Miss Scott is not used to drinking wine with every meal, Luis,' said Sanchia, regarding the other woman slightingly. 'The English drink tea, do they not? In great quantities, I believe.'

'Then you must allow me to take you on a tour of my family's vineyard,' said Luis at once, watching Enrique refill his glass. 'I can teach you all there is to know about wine, Cassandra.'

'And about other things, too, no doubt,' put in Sanchia insidiously. 'But I hardly think Miss Scott will be here long enough to have time to visit La Calida, Luis. Is that not so, Miss Scott?'

'Her name is de Montoya,' declared Enrique harshly, before

Luis could answer her, unable to deny the automatic reproof.
'Cassandra de Montoya. Or Señora de Montoya, if you will.
But not Miss Scott. I realise this is not easy for you, Sanchia,
but she is Antonio's widow. *Entiendes?* Do you understand?'

Sanchia sucked in her breath, but it was Cassandra who
saved her from taking offence at his words. 'I'm sure Señora
de Romero understands that very well,' she said firmly, although she still avoided looking at him. 'And she's right. I'm
sorry, Luis, but I don't think I will be able to accept your
invitation.'

'There, you see.' Now, Sanchia arched narrow eyebrows at
Enrique. 'Even your guest understands that she and her son
will be leaving soon.'

'That depends,' said Enrique, refilling his own glass, aware
that Cassandra had reacted to the challenge. He was drinking
too much, he thought, and the wine was loosening his tongue.

'That depends?' echoed Sanchia, determined to have her
way. 'When your father returns from the hospital, Enrique, he
will not want his home to be full of strangers, no?'

'Hardly strangers, Sanchia.' Enrique didn't know why he
was pursuing this. It wasn't as if he cared what she thought.
'Cassandra is my father's daughter-in-law; his *nuera*. And
David is his grandson. They are family.'

'But strangers, nonetheless,' insisted Sanchia, albeit a little
stiffly now. She paused. 'I did not realise you had told your
father that—that they are here. When I spoke with your
mother, she said that your father was unaware of David's existence.'

'But she is not,' said Enrique grimly, wondering when
Sanchia had spoken to his mother. What had Elena de
Montoya told her about their unexpected visitors? It infuriated
him that his mother might confide her feelings to Sanchia
when she'd scarcely spoken a word to Cassandra.

'In any case,' Sanchia continued quickly, as if she'd suddenly realised that allying herself with his mother might not
have been the wisest choice, 'I am sure discovering he has a
grandson may be exactly what your father needs to implement
his recovery.'

Are you? thought Enrique dourly, sure she didn't think any such thing. He scowled. Why was this evening going so badly wrong? Why, when his original intention in inviting Sanchia here had been to prove to himself that he and Cassandra had nothing in common, did he find her so much more appealing than the woman he'd known for half his life? And why was he spending his time defending her when it was towards Sanchia he should feel some remorse?

'I am sure when Julio meets Cassandra, he will be as enchanted with her as I am,' Luis inserted gallantly, evidently deciding the conversation was getting too heavy, and, setting down his glass, Enrique pushed back his chair.

'I think we should all adjourn to the *salón* for coffee,' he said non-committally, and then felt another twinge of irritation at Sanchia's smug expression. He crossed to the sideboard where a bell-cord summoned a waiting manservant. 'Is that agreeable to everyone?'

Cassandra folded her napkin and laid it beside her plate. But it was Luis who answered him. 'It is okay with me, *amigo*,' he said, getting to his feet. 'It will give me time to persuade Cassandra that La Calida is only an hour's drive from here.' He smiled down at her. 'What do you say, *cara*?'

'I think I should go and check on David,' she responded, lifting her head, looking at him, not at Enrique. 'If you'll excuse me...'

'*Pero*—'

'I will come with you,' said Enrique, pre-empting any offer Luis might have made to accompany her, earning an annoyed look from both his other guests. The arrival of a dark-coated retainer prevented any argument, however, and he ordered coffee to be served in the Salón de Alcazar. Then, before Cassandra could think of any objection, 'Make yourselves comfortable. We will not be long.'

'There's no need for anyone to come with me,' declared Cassandra shortly, as he followed her towards the door, and he heard the tremor in her voice she was trying hard to disguise. She looked up at him now and there were tears of outrage as well as anger in her eyes. 'Really, I would prefer to go alone.'

'And lose your way back?' he suggested in a low voice that only she could hear, and she pressed her hands together as if to the quell the urge to scratch his eyes out.

'I'm not completely stupid,' she said, her lips tight. She looked at the other woman, who was watching them with hard resentful eyes. 'If I don't see you again, Señora de Romero, it's been a—singular pleasure.'

Sanchia was taken aback. Enrique guessed she'd thought Cassandra was too intimidated by her surroundings to notice her veiled hostility, but she'd been wrong. They'd all been wrong about Cassandra, he admitted wryly. Including himself.

But he had the advantage in that this was his father's house and as his guest Cassandra could hardly order him not to go with her. Nevertheless, she set a brisk pace along the corridor that linked the family apartments with the other areas of the house and he was forced to quicken his step to keep up with her.

He didn't know how she walked as fast as she did in the high-heeled sandals she was wearing this evening; high heeled sandals that drew his attention to the slim ankles appearing below the hem of her long skirt. Her stride gave tantalising glimpses of the pale thighs exposed as her long steps parted the wrap-around folds.

He'd wished earlier that she'd worn a shorter skirt until he'd seen the way Luis was looking at her. Sanchia was wearing a short chiffon gown that displayed her silk-covered thighs to advantage, but the sequinned vest Cassandra had teamed with the ankle-length skirt was revealing enough. He'd found he objected to the other man ogling her narrow shoulders and slim arms, and he'd known a quite uncharacteristic desire to behave as his ancestors might have done and shut her away from any male eyes but his own.

Which was not something he wanted to think about at this moment. He tried to convince himself that his only motive in offering to accompany her was, as he'd said, to ensure that she found her way back. But now that they were alone together all he could think about was his own intense attraction to her. His hand went out almost involuntarily to fasten around her upper arm.

'Slow down!'

'I don't want to slow down.' Cassandra glanced scornfully at him. 'If you don't like the way I'm walking, why don't you do us both a favour and stop embarrassing me?'

'Embarrassing you?' Enrique exerted himself and brought her to a halt. 'How am I embarrassing you?'

'By behaving as if I'm not capable of finding my own way about the *palacio*.' Cassandra looked pointedly at his hand gripping her arm. 'I found my way here, didn't I? You have no right to do this.'

'In my culture, escorting a guest to her room is not considered to be embarrassing her,' retorted Enrique stiffly.

'Well, in mine, forcing your company on someone else is considered harassment,' replied Cassandra tersely. 'I wish you would leave me alone.'

Enrique didn't know how to answer that. She had every right to resent his actions and he would find it very hard to explain to himself why he was persisting with this. Far better to let her go and return to the others, to Sanchia, who would welcome him back with open arms. Why was he pursuing Cassandra when he'd already stirred up a storm by kissing her in the courtyard the morning his mother had arrived at the *palacio*? What did he want from her, for God's sake? Why didn't he just put the past behind him and let her go?

The truth was, he didn't want to let her go. And he was finding it far too easy to delude himself that she felt the same. If David *was* his son... But that way lay madness. David was Antonio's child. She'd told him so herself.

Or had she?

He looked down at her flesh beneath his hand and knew a surge of emotion. He liked holding her; he liked the warmth the connection was generating throughout the rest of his body. He liked the sense that she was his prisoner, though that was not a thought he wanted to pursue. But he liked the contrast between his dark tan and her much paler skin, the notion that, like the warp and weft of the tapestries behind him, they belonged together.

Trying not to look at the too-tempting beauty of her mouth, he said, 'I thought you might be glad of my company.' He spread a hand to encompass the long corridor with its high vaulted ceiling and sombre portraits of his ancestors. 'The Galería de los Inocentes can feel intimidating at night. I used to feel ghostly eyes watching me when I was a child.'

'But I'm not a child.' Cassandra glanced indifferently about her and he realised she had been too incensed by his behaviour to notice her surroundings. Now she acknowledged his words with a careless shrug of her shoulders. 'I'd say these paintings are more likely to haunt you than me. I've done nothing to arouse their—disapproval.'

'And I have?'

Her words provoked him. He was attempting to convince her that his motives were genuine, and all she was doing was trying to pick a fight.

'Haven't you?' she countered now, her voice low and scornful. 'Why don't you go back to your guests, Enrique? Whatever you say, Señora de Romero obviously considers she has some prior claim to your affections and I wouldn't like her to suspect that there was anything between us. Except contempt, of course.'

'*Maldita sea!* Damn you!' The words were wrung from him in spite of himself. It was hardly a surprise to learn that she had noticed Sanchia's proprietary attitude towards him but he resented the indifference she displayed. 'There is nothing between Sanchia and myself. Nothing!'

'If you say so.'

Patently she didn't believe him, and Enrique's patience grew close to breaking point. In the name of God, he thought, didn't she realise he had feelings? That when he was with her, he couldn't think about anyone else, let alone admit to a previous liaison?

'It's the truth,' he said, grasping her shoulder with his free hand and forcing her to face him. '*Bien*, perhaps we did turn to one another in the past, but it did not mean anything to either of us.'

'Like when you slept with me? That didn't mean anything to you either, did it?' she asked through suddenly tight lips, and he groaned aloud at the chasm he'd inadvertently dug for himself.

'Not like that, no.'

'Are you sure?'

Her eyes were glistening in the muted illumination from a dozen shaded wall-lights and for a moment he thought she was exulting in her victory. But then he realised that the shimmering between her burnished lashes was caused by tears and with an exclamation of remorse he gathered her into his arms.

'*Querida mia,*' he breathed unsteadily against her lips. Then, capturing her mouth with his, he pushed his tongue greedily into the moist yielding cavern that opened up for him. '*Te deseo*—I want you,' he found himself confessing as he had said once before. '*Tocame, cariña!* Touch me! *Dejame*— Let me—'

He sensed she wanted to resist him. The tears were now spilling down her cheeks. But although her hands came to grip his wrists, as if she would push him away from her, her lips told a different story. When he drew back to take a breath, she made a protesting little sound and sought his mouth again, twining her tongue with his and pressing her slim frame against him.

Enrique swayed back against the wall behind him, uncaring of the chill that shivered his spine. He took her with him, his hands sliding possessively from her shoulders to her hips, caressing the inch of skin that bared her navel. He didn't care that she must be able to feel the hard thrust of his arousal. As he rubbed himself against her he was speculating on the very real possibility that he might have to have her here, in the *galería*, with all the disapproving faces of his ancestors looking down at them. He'd never felt such desire for any woman except Cassandra, and the knowledge that she had been his brother's wife was like a knife that tore him apart.

His mouth captured hers again and he sucked on her lips,

drawing a moan of intense pleasure from deep inside him. She ought to have been his, he thought frustratedly, as the ache between his legs grew ever more insistent. She was his; he wanted her. And if his penance was that he should have recognised that fact sooner, then he was more than ready to pay the price.

His mouth moved from hers, along the silken curve of her cheek and jawline to the scented hollow of her throat. He slid the strap of the sequinned vest aside to taste the luscious skin of her neck, knowing as he did so that he wanted to bite her, to devour her, to make her his woman, his beloved, his *amante*...

'Enrique,' she whispered weakly, but it was hardly a protest. Even when he parted her skirt with his thigh and slipped his fingers into the soft folds, she didn't object. Beneath the hem of her lacy panties, which were all she was wearing under the skirt, a pulse beat against his fingers. Damp curls guarded the quivering core of her womanhood, and when he pressed between, he found her wet and ready for him. 'My God, Enrique,' she gulped. 'What are you doing to me?'

'I think you know what you are doing to me, *querida*,' he countered breathlessly, his lungs labouring for air as his fingertips probed the slick honeycomb of muscles he'd found. He couldn't prevent a groan of satisfaction. '*Dios*, Cassandra, I should never have let you marry Antonio. You were mine before you were his. David should have been my son. Mine! How could I have been such a fool as to let you go?'

He heard her catch her breath, felt the sudden shudder that rippled over her body and for a moment he thought it was a response to his stroking fingers. But then, with an agonised cry, she tore herself away from him.

'Don't say that!' she said on a choking breath. 'Don't dare pretend that what passed between us was anything more than a brutal attempt on your part to break us—Antonio and me— to break us up!'

Enrique muffled an oath. 'You do not understand,' he said roughly, pushing himself away from the wall and making a futile attempt to capture her again. 'Cassandra, listen to me.

Why do you think I left for Spain before the wedding? Because I could not bear to see you with him! As God is my witness, I have not been able to think of you and he together without it tearing me apart.'

Cassandra shook her head, staring at him with wide disbelieving eyes, her cheeks still stained with the tears she had shed earlier. 'Oh, you're good, I'll give you that,' she said bitterly. 'If I didn't know better, I'd almost be prepared to believe that you mean what you say.'

'I do mean it,' protested Enrique harshly. '*Dios*, Cassandra, it is the truth. Ever since I found out about David, I have suffered the pains of Hades! If I had only realised what I had, what I was losing, you would have been my wife! David would have been my son!'

'He is your son.'

The words were spoken so softly, barely audibly in fact, that Enrique thought for a moment that he had imagined them. Yet he was so wired by his emotions he knew he would have heard a pin drop.

He swallowed. 'What did you say?'

Cassandra trembled, and he could tell from her expression that she was already regretting her impulsiveness. 'Nothing,' she said now, her eyes wide and apprehensive. 'I made a mistake.' She glanced fearfully about her. 'I—I have to go—'

'Not yet.' Enrique moved with more speed than he would have thought he was capable of a moment ago and stepped into her path, barring her way. His eyes narrowed incredulously, his desire for her being stifled by raw disbelief. 'What do you mean by saying something like that? David is Antonio's child.' He took a steadying breath. 'He must be.'

'Must he?' Cassandra hesitated, but then it seemed she'd decided to bluff it out. She held up her head with a touching air of dignity. 'Yes, you're probably right.'

Her vulnerability tore at him, but he refused to allow himself to be distracted by the anxiety he could see in her eyes. In God's name, why was she lying? Did she believe David was his son or not?

'Why would you say a thing like that?' he demanded, the

harshness of his tone belying the uncertainty he was feeling. 'Dammit, Cassandra, are you playing with me? Do you not think I have suffered enough for that one mistake?'

'You've suffered?' Her voice broke and she struggled to control herself. 'Oh, Enrique, you have no idea what it means to feel pain. I—I was a virgin when you made love to me,' she reminded him tremulously. 'Did it never occur to you that there might be consequences for what you did?'

Enrique stared at her. 'You are saying he is my son?' He was staggered. 'But how do you know that? What proof do you have?'

'Proof?' Cassandra gazed at him pityingly. 'I don't need any proof,' she told him painfully. 'You know what happened as well as I do. Antonio died on the day we were married. Thank God, he never had the chance to—to discover what you'd done.'

CHAPTER TWELVE

DAVID came into Cassandra's bedroom the next morning with a sullen expression marring his good-looking features. For one awful moment, his mother wondered if Enrique had been talking to him about what had happened the night before, but David's first words were reassuring.

'Tio Enrique's gone,' he muttered, slouching moodily about her room for a few minutes before subsiding onto the end of her bed. 'Carlos says he doesn't know when he'll be back. Do you think he's sick of us? Do you think he's hoping we'll be gone before he comes home?'

Cassandra refrained from pointing out that Tuarega was not strictly Enrique's home. It would be his one day, and telling David that his uncle—his *father*—had a house further up the valley was not wise. He might well decide to go and see if Enrique was there and she had enough to worry about without fretting about her son's whereabouts, too.

She still couldn't quite believe what she'd done. She'd hardly slept, and she'd been lying here for the past few hours trying to understand why she'd been so stupid. Now, hearing that Enrique had left the *palacio*, she knew she ought to feel grateful. He was giving her time to come to terms with the situation, she thought tensely. Or would Enrique be so considerate? Might it not be the case that he had gone away because he didn't believe her? Perhaps he thought she had some idea of using her son to her advantage. By saying he was his son and not Antonio's, she had obviously strengthened David's claim to be Julio de Montoya's heir.

She felt sick. Surely he couldn't think she was as mercenary as that? She hadn't wanted to come here. She'd wanted nothing from the de Montoyas. But, whichever way she looked at it, she had given Enrique unwarranted power over her; over

133

both of them. Dared she wait and see what he chose to do with it?

And this was all because she hadn't been able to control her hormones, she thought bitterly. Because Enrique had kissed her and stroked her, and brought her to the brink of orgasm with his caressing hands, she'd been deluded into thinking that what they were sharing was real, was honest, that it meant the same to him as it did to her.

God, what a fool she'd been!

Enrique had wanted her. He'd wanted to have sex with her, but that was all. All evening, he'd watched her with his dark, hooded eyes, mentally undressing her with his sensual glances. Glances that had brought the hot blood coursing to the surface of her skin and caused liquid heat to pool between her thighs.

How had she known what he was thinking? Because, however much he might resent the fact, he was attracted to her. Physically attracted, she amended. He had desired to bury his hard flesh within hers. And it might have come to that if she hadn't been so reckless; if she hadn't opened her mouth and confessed the secret she'd been guarding all these years.

'Do you know where he's gone?' asked David suddenly, misinterpreting her silence, and Cassandra realised she was in danger of allowing him to see that something was wrong.

'Why would I?' she countered, propping herself up on her elbows and pushing the heavy weight of her hair out of her eyes. She forced a smile. 'Have you had breakfast?'

'I thought he might have said something last night,' persisted David, not interested in her attempt to change the subject, and Cassandra's lips parted.

'Last—night?'

Her voice faltered but David didn't appear to notice her hesitation. 'You had dinner with him and his friends, didn't you?' he demanded impatiently. 'He must have said something.'

'Not about going away,' said Cassandra, throwing back the sheet and sliding her legs out of bed with more determination than enthusiasm.

In fact, Enrique had said nothing after her assertion that she and Antonio had never consummated their marriage. After one stunned look in her direction, he'd turned and walked away, and she'd been left with the cold conviction that she had destroyed any chance of them ever forgiving one another for the past.

'I bet he's gone away with that woman,' grumbled David now, getting up from the bed and dragging his feet across to the open balcony doors. 'Is he going to marry her, do you think?' He hunched his shoulders and rested his arms on the balcony rail, his back to the room. 'I hope not.'

'Why?' Cassandra couldn't prevent the question and David turned to give her an old-fashioned look. 'What?' she protested. 'I don't know what you're talking about.'

'Oh, Mum!' David gave her a pitying look. 'Don't you see? If Tio Enrique marries someone else, he won't care about us any more. He'll have a wife, maybe a family. We'll just be the poor relations.'

Cassandra swallowed. 'If he marries *someone else*?' she echoed faintly. 'I didn't know he'd been married.'

'He hasn't,' exclaimed David impatiently. 'I meant, instead of you. Surely you've thought about it, too?'

'Thought about what?' Cassandra refused to put words to what he was suggesting.

'About marrying Tio Enrique,' replied her son at once. 'It's the ideal solution. Dad's dead and you don't have anyone else. We could be a real family. You and me and—'

'No!' The word was strangled and Cassandra gazed at him with horrified eyes. He was truly his father's child, she thought bleakly. He didn't hesitate. He went straight for the jugular. 'You don't know what you're talking about,' she protested. 'I—Enrique de Montoya would never marry me!'

The fact that she'd entertained such a thought herself last night when he'd been making love to her was not something she cared to share with him. Not that or what had come after. Remembering the way Enrique had looked at her before he strode away, she wondered if she was a fool in thinking he'd ever want to speak to her again.

'Why not?' David wasn't prepared to give up that easily.

He came back into the room. He caught his mother's cold hands in his, pulling her up from the bed and gazing at her as if he'd just solved the secret of the universe. 'You're young. You're quite pretty, even if you are nearly thirty.' He made thirty sound like middle age. 'You need someone to—to look after you.'

'No, David.'

He scowled, and then flung her hands away from him. 'You always say that,' he exclaimed unfairly. 'Whatever I want to do, you always have a better idea.'

'That's not true.' Cassandra was defensive.

'Yes, it is.' He pushed his hands into the pockets of his baggy shorts. 'You didn't want to come here, did you? And if you'd known I'd written that letter to Grandpapa, you'd have stopped me from sending it, too.'

Cassandra sighed. 'David, you don't understand—'

'No, I don't,' he muttered sulkily. 'You like it here. I know you do. All right, maybe Grandmama wasn't very friendly, but you can't blame her.'

'Can't I?' Cassandra's voice was faint with dismay.

'No.' David sniffed. 'I mean, what did you expect? They didn't even know they had a grandson.'

Cassandra's lips parted. 'How do you know that?' she asked, sure Enrique must have told him, but David was nothing if not honest.

'It was Juan, actually,' he said, having the grace to look slightly discomfited now. 'He told me.'

'Juan?' Cassandra shook her head in bewilderment. She'd never imagined that their affairs might be common knowledge among the estate staff. But she supposed she should have known better. She steeled herself for the worst. 'So what did he tell you?'

David hunched his shoulders. 'Not a lot.'

'David!'

He hesitated. 'He said that no one at Tuarega had known that Señor Antonio had a son. He—he said that if they had, Grandpapa would have—would have brought me to live with him.'

'Did he?' Cassandra found she was trembling and she wrapped her arms about her midriff, hugging herself tightly. 'And what was your response to that?'

David shrugged. 'I don't remember.' His mother stared at him, but this time he refused to budge. 'I don't,' he insisted defensively. 'I—I thought at first that he must have made a mistake.'

Cassandra moistened her lips. 'And when did you decide he hadn't?'

'I guess I just worked it out for myself,' muttered David unhappily. 'I think Tio Enrique would have come to see us if he'd known. Why wouldn't he? Juan says that family is really important to the de Montoyas. And we are family.'

'You are,' said Cassandra flatly, unable to continue with this. Her worst fears had been realised. Not only did David believe he knew who he was, but he blamed her for his estrangement from his father's family. Oh, he hadn't said so, not in so many words. But it was just a matter of time and then...

'You're family, too,' protested David, suddenly seeming to realise that this wasn't going at all the way he'd expected. 'Mum!' This as she turned away and began taking clean underwear out of a drawer, preparatory to taking her morning shower. 'Look, I'm sorry if I've upset you. But, honestly, I really think you've got this all wrong.'

'Do you?' With fresh shorts and a sleeveless tanktop draped over her arm, Cassandra paused in the doorway to the bathroom. 'Well, you're entitled to your opinion, of course. But David, believe me, Enrique de Montoya isn't interested in me. In you, yes. As you say, you're—family. As far as I'm concerned the de Montoyas made it very clear ten years ago that they wanted nothing to do with me. Right?'

'But they didn't know about me,' exclaimed David, following her across the room, and Cassandra gave him a disbelieving look.

'Do you think that makes a difference?' she demanded, and once again, he looked shamefaced.

'I—don't know.'

'Well, it doesn't,' said Cassandra tightly, and unable to hide her feelings any longer, she did the unthinkable and slammed the door in his face.

'Mum!'

David was hurt. He wasn't used to being treated this way, but Cassandra didn't give in to his pleas. With the lock secured and her shoulders pressed against the door for good measure, she gave in to the emotions that had been threatening for the past few hours. Ignoring her son's agitated rattling of the handle, she allowed the hot tears to stream unchecked down her cheeks, and not until David had given up and gone away did she make any attempt to do what she'd come into the bathroom for.

Enrique had always thought that Seville was the most Spanish of cities. It was also one of the most beautiful places in Spain, some might say in the world, and he'd always loved it.

But today even the sight of its famous cathedral did little to lift his spirits. The huge Gothic church and the Giralda tower, which was the city's most famous landmark, were just monuments to a way of life that he didn't want to identify with any more.

Cassandra's words had cut deeply into the fabric of his existence. The devastating realisation that for the last ten years he had been living a lie left him feeling sick and bewildered. Although he wanted to deny it, to accuse her of using one mistake to justify her actions, he knew in his heart of hearts that she was telling the truth.

The boy was his. David was his; the child he had so instantly recognised as being his own flesh and blood was in reality so much more. Flesh of his flesh; blood of his blood; fruit of his genes, of his loins. The son he had never expected to have.

And Cassandra's, he added tensely. Though there was no chance of him forgetting that. He gave a snort of disgust. God, and he had blamed her for keeping the child a secret from them! She must have spent the last ten years hating him, hating his father, hating the very name of de Montoya. No wonder she had been so shocked when he had turned up at the *pensión* in Punta del Lobo. He must have been the very last person she wanted to see.

If David hadn't written that letter...

But he couldn't think about that now. He had other, arguably more important, matters to attend to. His father was due to leave the hospital tomorrow and his mother had requested him to come and drive the old man home to Tuarega. She had asked him to come today because she wanted all the formalities dealt with in advance of her husband's release date; or so she'd said. But Enrique suspected that she still hadn't told Julio about David and she wanted him to tell his father before he arrived at the *palacio* and discovered the truth for himself.

It was still early when he arrived at the block of apartments where his mother was staying. Not yet ten o'clock, and already he felt as if he had done a day's work. He hadn't eaten since Cassandra's revelation of the night before; hadn't slept. And now, faced with the prospect of telling his mother who David really was, he felt hopelessly unequal to the task.

Yet strangely elated, too, he realised, parking the Mercedes in the shade of a huge flowering acacia. Its yellow blossoms dripped feathery shadows over the car and as Enrique got out he inhaled the distinctive aromas of heat and vegetation and the unavoidable smell of exhaust fumes that hung in the languid air.

The de Montoya *apartamento* occupied the top floor of the five-storey building that overlooked the formal gardens of one of the city's parks. After exchanging a few words with the doorman, Enrique took one of the old-fashioned elevators up to the penthouse. A padded bench furnished the small panelled cubicle and hand-operated wrought-iron gates replaced the efficient sliding doors he was used to but Enrique scarcely noticed. Everything about the building proclaimed its age and conservatism, but his parents liked it and there was no doubt that, when any of the apartments became vacant, there was always a list of would-be tenants waiting to move in.

Bonita, his mother's housemaid, let him in, her plump face exhibiting her surprise at his early arrival. 'Señora de Montoya is not yet up, *señor*,' she explained, following him into a spacious salon whose long windows gave a magnificent view of the cathedral. 'I will tell her you are here.'

'There's no hurry, Bonita,' he replied, glancing about him at the familiar surroundings of the apartment. Heavy carved furniture, richly coloured upholstery echoed in the thick drapes hanging at the windows: the room was a mirror-image of the apartments his parents occupied at the *palacio* but without its height and space to mitigate the oppressive effect. 'I'll have some coffee while I wait.'

'Yes, *señor*.'

Bonita bustled away to do his bidding and Enrique moved to the windows, standing with his hands pushed into the hip pockets of his black trousers, the collar of his dark green shirt gaping open to expose the hair-roughened skin of his throat. The apartment was air-conditioned and he was grateful for it. He'd begun to feel the heat coming up in the elevator.

'Enrique!'

His mother's voice disturbed him. Turning, he found her standing just inside the door that led to the inner hall of the apartment, a lavender-coloured velvet robe wrapped tightly about her, as if she was cold.

Judging by her expression, Enrique apprehended that she thought his early arrival heralded bad news and he hurried to reassure her. 'Mamá,' he said, going to her and bestowing a kiss on her dry cheek. 'How are you? All ready to return to Tuarega?'

'As I'll ever be,' declared Elena de Montoya shortly. 'I take it you are eager to tell your father what you've done? That is why you are here before breakfast, I assume?'

'You haven't told him?' Enrique knew it was a pointless question. Obviously she hadn't or she would have said so.

'No.' Elena gathered the folds of the robe at her throat and gave him a haughty look. 'You brought that woman and her son to Tuarega, Enrique. It is your duty to tell your father who they are.'

'They are your daughter-in-law and your grandson, Mamá,' retorted Enrique, feeling the nerves coiling tightly in his stomach. 'You cannot dispute that.'

His mother drew a deep breath. 'The boy is a de Montoya,' she agreed. 'Of that there is no doubt.'

'Then?'

'But he has not been brought up as a de Montoya, Enrique,' she exclaimed impatiently. 'As he would have been if he had been your son.'

'He is my son, Mamá.'

It was as easy as that. The words simply formed themselves and before he could consider their impact they had slipped out, as clear and as damning as the conviction behind them.

His mother stared at him blankly for a moment. Her eyes dilated, mirroring the numbing effect of his words, and it was apparent that she was in a state of shock.

He would have gone to her then but she waved him away, moving to the armchair nearest to her and groping for its support. Like a much older woman than she actually was, she lowered herself onto the cushioned seat and sat for several seconds just gazing at him as if she'd never seen him before.

Then, when his own skin was feeling clammily damp with sweat, she spoke again. 'Why didn't you tell me this before?'

'As you told me you had discussed David's future with Sanchia?' Enrique sighed. 'I didn't know before last night.'

His mother avoided his question and asked one of her own. 'You expect me to believe that?'

'It's the truth.'

'But you must have—'

'No.' Enrique's nostrils flared. 'No, I didn't. How could I? You know how Cassandra feels about me, about us. She didn't even want to come here, to Spain. That was David's idea; the letter was David's idea. If he hadn't written to Papá...'

'We would never have known of his existence,' said his mother faintly, and Enrique nodded. 'But why not? Surely she must have known how we would have felt if we'd known she was expecting a child?'

'My child?' suggested Enrique drily, and his mother came unsteadily to her feet.

'Your child,' she said incredulously. Then, with harsh emphasis, 'How could you, Enrique? How could you? Your own brother's wife!'

'She wasn't his wife when—when we—'

'Spare me all the sordid details,' exclaimed Elena, shaking her head in distaste. 'I cannot believe this, Enrique. All the time that I was at Tuarega; all those hours I spent talking with David, believing he was Antonio's child.'

Enrique shrugged. 'I am sorry.'

'Sorry?' His mother looked up at him with bitter eyes. 'Sorry does not even begin to cover it.' She paused. 'But how do you know that woman—Cassandra—is not lying? How can you be sure that David is *your* son?'

'He is,' said Enrique flatly.

'But how—?'

'She was a virgin when I made love to her,' replied Enrique harshly, and his mother winced. 'She and Antonio never had the chance to consummate their marriage. He was killed only hours after the wedding, remember?'

'How could I forget?' asked Elena bleakly, and then glanced round apprehensively when Bonita came back carrying a tray of coffee and freshly squeezed orange juice.

The housemaid greeted her mistress warmly, setting the tray on the table nearest to where she was sitting before turning to Enrique. 'Some toast or a croissant, perhaps, *señor*?' she suggested. 'I have some home-made strawberry conserve.'

'The coffee will do, Bonita,' he replied with a small smile. 'Thank you.'

'And you, *señora*?'

'Nothing, nothing.' Elena waved an agitated hand at the housemaid. 'Leave us.' This as the woman went to pour the coffee. 'My son can take care of it. He seems to think he can handle everything else.'

'Yes, *señora*.'

Bonita withdrew, but not before she had exchanged a startled look with Enrique, and after she had gone he pulled a wry face. 'There's no need to take your feelings out on the staff,' he remarked reprovingly. 'It's not Bonita's fault that you're stressed.'

Elena's lips tightened. 'Nor mine either,' she reminded him tightly. 'And please don't use that language in my presence. You are a de Montoya, Enrique. That should mean something to you.'

'It does,' he said flatly. 'It means arrogance, and pride, and an overwhelming belief in one's own importance in the scheme of things. But do you know what, Mamá? All of a sudden that sounds awfully hollow to me.'

'Because you've just found out that you have a son you never knew?' she demanded contemptuously. 'We all make mistakes, Enrique. Even you.'

'Yes, we do,' he agreed, suddenly wanting to be out of the apartment and away from this dried-up old woman who always believed she was right. 'But you'll never guess what my mistake was. Never in a million years!'

CHAPTER THIRTEEN

ENRIQUE didn't return to Tuarega that evening.

Cassandra had spent the morning in a state of extreme agitation, sure he would want more of an explanation than she had given him the night before and steeling herself to face his anger. But her lunch had been served without any explanation being given for his departure, and she consoled herself with the thought that the longer he stayed away, the shorter time there would be left for them to remain at the *palacio* when he got back.

She was reluctant to consider what he might be thinking. If he had believed her, she didn't want to contemplate what his actions might be. No matter how attractive the proposition, the possibility that he might have dismissed what she'd told him as pure fabrication became more and more unlikely as each hour passed. He'd believed her, she thought sickly, and now she had to ponder how she was going to deal with it.

The most attractive option was to leave Tuarega. The idea of calling a cab, of loading herself and David into it and driving to the airport to catch a flight back to England, was almost irresistible. But she couldn't do that. Apart from anything else, she doubted David would want to go with her, and, while she could override his wishes, sooner or later she was going to have to face the consequences of what she'd done.

Why had she done it? she had asked herself again that afternoon, having left the *palacio* in search of her son and found herself standing at the rail of one of the paddocks where some of Enrique's bulls had been grazing the lush grass. Why had she told him? No one had forced her hand. However loath she might be to admit it, hadn't she secretly just been waiting for a chance to cut the ground out from under him? To wipe the smug smile from his face once and for all?

144

She had shuddered, wrapping her arms about herself as the cold suspicion took root. She didn't want to admit that she'd found any pleasure in telling him. She hadn't, she assured herself fiercely. But she must have hurt him and that was an emotion she could identify with very well.

'*Señora?*'

It had been Carlos, his lined face wearing an anxious expression, and Cassandra had wondered if Enrique had confided in him before taking off for God knew where.

'Hi,' she said, forcing a smile. And then, nodding towards the bulls, one or two of whom had lifted their heads and were regarding them with disconcerting interest. 'I was just admiring the stock.'

'*Sí, señora.*' Although Carlos spoke a little English he understood considerably more and he looked at the powerful herd with a certain amount of pride. Then, with a shrug, 'But you do not like *los toros*, no?'

Cassandra tried to be objective. 'I have nothing against the animals exactly…'

'But you do not like the—um—bullfight, *sí*?'

'*Sí,*' agreed Cassandra, resting her elbows on the rail and gazing at the bulls with doubtful eyes. 'It's—cruel.'

'Ah, *cruel.*' Carlos used the Spanish pronunciation. 'Many things are *cruel*, *señora.*' He paused. '*El toro* dies a—how would you say?—a death *valeroso*, no?'

'A valiant death? No.' Cassandra was diverted from her own problems by his teasing provocation. 'The bull dies in pain; in agony. It bleeds to death, doesn't it?'

'Ah, no.' Carlos lifted one finger and shook it from side to side. '*El torero*, he kills with *la estocada*. His sword. Into the neck, so!'

'I'd rather not hear the details.' Cassandra shivered and the old man smiled.

'Señor Enrique: he was like you when he was younger.'

'Enrique?' She couldn't believe it.

'*Pero, sí.*' Carlos watched one of the bulls that was approaching them with wary eyes. 'Even today, he does not attend the *corrida, señora*. These are his bulls; his *toros bravos*.

But he has no wish to know what happens to them after they leave, *entiende usted*?'

Cassandra shook her head, remembering what she had said to Enrique, what she'd accused him of. Dear God, was there no part of their relationship that had not suffered from misunderstandings? Was she always to feel the ignominy of being in the wrong?

'Come, *señora*.' Carlos indicated the bull which was now only a few feet away and was watching them with sharp beady eyes. 'We would not want to offend *nuestros companeros*, no? Let me escort you back to the *palacio*. Señor Enrique would never forgive me if anything happened to you.'

Cassandra went with him, but she doubted Enrique cared what happened to her. From his point of view, it would make his life considerably less complicated if she were to go back to England. Alone, of course. After her revelations, he would have even more reason to want to keep David here.

David himself was another matter. She didn't honestly know how her son would react if he was given the choice. He loved her; of course he did. But he loved being here, at Tuarega. And it was bound to be a temptation if Enrique explained that it would all be his some day.

Depression enveloped her. All this, and she still hadn't taken into account how her son would feel when he learned the truth. Would he blame her for keeping him from his father? Would he ever understand her dilemma after the way the de Montoyas had treated her?

Somehow, she doubted it. In David's world, things were either black or white, bad or good, and telling lies did not come naturally to him. It was one of the things she had always loved about him. His candour, and his honesty; his willingness to take the blame if he was at fault. But he wasn't at fault now. She was. And she didn't know what to do about it.

Then, that evening, she got a call from her father.

She'd left a forwarding address with the proprietor of the *pensión* where they'd stayed in Punta del Lobo, mainly because she hadn't wanted to phone her father and tell him where they were going. She'd known Mr Scott wouldn't approve and

it would have taken too long to explain the situation to him.
Or that was what she'd told herself. Foolishly, she'd imagined
that all explanations could wait until they got home, but now
it seemed her father had decided to ring and assure himself
that all was well and they hadn't been there.

'What's going on, Cass?' he demanded, as soon as she came
on the line. 'I thought you told me you had no intention of
contacting Antonio's family.'

'I didn't,' said Cassandra quickly, aware of David standing
behind her, listening to every word. 'I—David wanted to meet
them.' She glanced over her shoulder. 'He's here. Do you want
to have a word with him?'

'No, I want to know why you'd go to Tuarega without telling me where you were,' retorted her father shortly. 'For
heaven's sake, Cass! Don't I deserve an explanation?'

'Of course you do.' Cassandra sighed, and David came to
stand by her shoulder. 'Look, we can't talk on the phone.
We'll be home in a few days. I'll tell you all about it then.'

'Is that Grandad?' asked David, catching on. 'Let me say
hello.'

'In a minute.' Cassandra felt as if she was wedged between
a rock and a hard place. 'Dad, give me the chance to explain.'

'Explain what?' He was angry. 'You had all this planned,
didn't you, Cass? You knew exactly what you were going to
do before you left England. All that talk about worrying
whether the de Montoyas might find out where you were was
all—rubbish, wasn't it?'

'No.' Cassandra was hurt that he should think so. 'I had no
idea that David—'

She broke off, not wanting to tell him what her son had
done, but her father wouldn't leave it there.

'You had no idea that David—what?' Mr Scott snorted.
'You're not going to tell me that this was his idea?'

'It was.' Cassandra sighed again. 'Here: I'll put him on. He
can tell you about it himself.'

David took the phone eagerly, and before his grandfather
could speak, he exclaimed, 'You ought to see this place,
Grandad! It's fantastic! It's got a gym and a swimming pool,

and as well as the horses that Tio Enrique rides there are about a hundred bulls! They're great! A bit scary, sometimes, but Tio Enrique says that so long as you're careful, they won't hurt you.'

'David, David!' Cassandra could hear her father trying to calm him down. 'Let me speak to your mother again, will you, son? I'll hear all about the holiday when you get back.'

David's face dropped. 'But Grandad—'

'Not now, David.' Cassandra knew her father was having difficulty in controlling his temper. 'Put your mother on. This call is costing me a fortune.'

David handed the phone to Cassandra with ill grace. 'Here,' he said, pushing his hands into the pockets of his shorts and staring defiantly at her. 'Why should I speak to him anyway? He's never been interested in what I do.'

'That's not true,' protested Cassandra, horrified, covering the phone with her hand. 'David, your grandfather has always cared about your welfare. Where would we have been without him, that's what I'd like to know? Don't be such a baby. He's worried because we'd left the *pensión* without telling him, that's all.' She paused. 'Go and get your pyjamas on. It's nearly time for bed.'

David left the room without speaking and she hoped she was not going to have to mediate between him and her father. She seemed to be spending her time lurching from one crisis to another, and it seemed to be the pattern at the moment for her to be the scapegoat for everyone's grievances.

Somehow, she managed to placate her father without telling him about David's letter. She sensed that that would infuriate him still more, and, after assuring Mr Scott that in an emergency she would do as he suggested and use her credit card to get an earlier flight home, she managed to end the call. But he wasn't satisfied, she knew that, and he would demand a full explanation when she got back. Someone else, she thought drily. How many more explanations would she have to make?

She awakened the next morning feeling more hungover than she'd done the previous day. She had slept; exhaustion had seen to that. But her sleep had been shallow and punctuated with nightmare scenes of David being pursued by one of Enrique's fighting bulls, its beady eyes red and glittering with malevolence.

She crawled out of bed feeling sick and headachy, her mouth tasting foul, and her skin sticky with the sweat her dreams had generated. Even a shower did little to lift her mood, and when she emerged from her bedroom to find David tucking into butter-slathered rolls and freshly squeezed orange juice, she thought how unfair life was.

'Hi, Mum,' he said, his expression considerably more cheerful than it had been the night before. 'I know where Tio Enrique is. He's in Seville. He's gone to fetch Grandpapa home. Isn't that exciting?'

Cassandra swallowed. Exciting wasn't the word she'd have used to describe her feelings at the thought of seeing Julio de Montoya again. She couldn't even claim to have *met* him before. A stiff black-suited figure at the service Cassandra had held for her late husband, he hadn't so much as exchanged a word with his daughter-in-law. He'd saved all his comments for the priest who'd conducted the service, and her nerves prickled at the thought of his anger when he discovered the secret she'd been keeping from them all these years.

'How do you know?' she asked obliquely, pouring herself a cup of the strong coffee Consuela had provided for them. Carlos had said nothing to her, but then the old man was always excessively discreet where his employer was concerned.

'Consuela told me,' David replied at once, helping himself to another roll. 'They'll be home later today. According to her, Grandpapa is leaving the hospital this morning. He'll be surprised to meet me, won't he?'

'No doubt.' Cassandra tried to keep the anxiety out of her voice. 'Um—just don't expect too much, will you, David? I mean, your grandfather's been very ill. He may need a few days to—to recover from the journey.'

David's eyes darkened with a mixture of doubt and resentment. 'But Tio Enrique said Grandpapa would be pleased to hear he had a grandson,' he protested peevishly. 'Are you sure that's not just you hoping we won't get on? I mean he is my dad's father. I think he'll be rapt when he knows we're here.'

Cassandra couldn't imagine Julio de Montoya being rapt about anything, least of all a grandson who was half her blood. She was still the outsider as far as he was concerned. And nothing that had happened since she arrived in Spain had given her any reason to think that that was likely to change.

Apparently preferring Juan's company to hers, David disappeared after breakfast and, left to herself, Cassandra decided to start packing their belongings. It would give her something to do, and although there were still a few more days before they were due back at Punta del Lobo to catch the bus which would take them to Seville airport, it made her feel as if she was doing something positive for a change.

It was early afternoon when she heard the car. She didn't want to admit that she'd been listening for it, but she had. She found herself going out into the sunlit courtyard and staring out across the wide sweep of the valley, wondering with a shameful sense of apprehension if Julio de Montoya would want to see her. Not today, she assured herself firmly. When he was rested, perhaps. She had no illusions as to who would bear the brunt of her father-in-law's wrath, but he must need time to recover his strength.

In fact it was less than an hour before she heard the sound of footsteps crossing the marble floor of the *salón*. Cassandra was still in her bedroom, pretending to be engrossed in sorting through the contents of her cosmetics bag, when a shadow filled the open doorway and she looked up to find Enrique standing there, watching her.

He was the very last person she had expected to see. Consuela, perhaps? David? But not Enrique. And yet, why not? It was appropriate, she thought bitterly. He was used to doing his father's bidding.

All the same, she couldn't meet his searching gaze for long. His absence had done nothing to damp the leaping fires inside her, and all she could remember was how weak and helpless he'd made her feel.

For his part, Enrique's face was expressionless, and she had no way of knowing what he was thinking. In a more formal shirt than she was used to seeing—ice-blue silk teamed with an Italian-styled suit in navy blue—he looked darkly handsome, disturbingly elegant. Her nemesis, she reflected a little shakily. Her fate and her temptation, and ultimately her destruction.

'If you're looking for David, he's not here,' she said, when the silence between them was beginning to strip her nerves. And Enrique shrugged.

'I can see that,' he replied, with no apparent inflection in his voice. 'What are you doing?'

'Nothing much.' Cassandra had been sitting on the padded stool beside the vanity, but now she got to her feet. There was no need for him to know she'd started packing. 'What do you want?'

Enrique rocked back on his heels. 'What do *I* want?' he queried, an edge of sarcasm colouring his tone. '*Dios*, where do I begin?'

Cassandra held up her head, not answering him. 'I understand you went to Seville to bring your father home,' she said instead, managing somehow to keep her voice cool and controlled. 'How is he? I expect he'll be tired after the journey.'

Enrique swore then. It wasn't in English, but Cassandra had no difficulty in identifying his intent. So much for hoping they could deal amicably with one another, she thought tensely. Like her, Enrique had not forgotten any part of what she'd said.

'Let us not pretend that you care how my father is feeling,' he said at last. 'And I understand perfectly what you are doing; what you are hoping to achieve. But it is not going to work, Cassandra. You and I are going to talk about what happened before I went away. You cannot tear my world apart and then behave as if nothing had changed. Even you are not that thoughtless.'

'Don't you mean stupid?' demanded Cassandra, stung by his accusation. 'And if you are going to talk about worlds being torn apart—'

'I know, I know.' Enrique dragged his hands out of his

pockets to rake long fingers through his hair. 'I have had time to think while I have been away and I realise it must have been—difficult—for you, too.'

'Oh, thanks.'

'Do not be sarcastic, Cassandra. It does not suit you.' He drew a steadying breath. 'In any case, now is not the time to get into this. It will take considerably longer than we have at present to deal with all the repercussions of this situation.'

Cassandra quivered. 'You're going away again?' she enquired tautly, and he uttered another muffled oath.

'No,' he said, leaving the door to cross the room towards her. He halted only when she put out her hand to prevent him from getting too close to her. '*Dios mío*, Cassandra, you must know how I feel. When you told me David was my son, I was shocked, yes. But it does not alter the way I feel about you.'

Cassandra moistened dry lips. 'Am I supposed to understand what that means?'

'You should,' he said roughly, taking the hand she had put out to stop him and raising it to his lips. 'I thought I made the way I felt about you very clear the other evening.'

'That was—that was before—'

'Before you told me that David was my son?' he enquired softly, his tongue devastatingly sensual against her palm. 'Ah, *sí*. And you do not think that that would reinforce those feelings?'

'I—don't know.' Cassandra didn't know what to believe any more.

'Then I will have to—'

But before he could finish what he'd been about to say, a throat was cleared behind them. '*Señor!*' It was Consuela. '*Lo siento, Señor Enrique,*' she murmured with obvious reluctance. '*Pero, señor, su padre—puede—*'

'*Mierda!*'

There was no mistaking Enrique's irritation now. With his jaw compressed in evident frustration, he dropped Cassandra's hand and turned to confront the red-faced maidservant, giving in to a stream of angry Spanish that was hardly warranted. And, although Cassandra could understand a little of his provocation, she couldn't help feeling sorry for Consuela, too. The Spanish woman wasn't to blame for the interruption. Someone else had sent her here.

Su padre. Your father. Cassandra translated the words without difficulty and her stomach tensed. Who else?

Enrique had apparently come to the same conclusion. He was being unreasonable, and, taking a deep breath, he shook his head. Recovering his temper, he offered the woman a swift apology, and this sudden reversal of blame brought a relieved smile to her lips. His words were eagerly accepted and Consuela hurried away, her rope-soled mules squeaking on the marble floor.

Listening, Cassandra was amazed they hadn't heard her coming. But perhaps that wasn't so surprising. For a few moments Enrique had had all her attention, and she was horrified to find that she was still so easily seduced.

Now, however, she had had time to gather her senses, and when he turned back to her, she was ready for him. 'I think you'd better go,' she said, trying not to show how upset he'd made her. 'I understood a little of what Consuela was saying. Your father is asking for you, isn't he? You'd better not keep him waiting.'

'As a matter of fact, it is you he is asking for, Cassandra,' Enrique declared, and there was an element of resignation in his voice now. 'He sent me here to bring you to him. He is eager to meet his daughter-in-law at last.'

Cassandra took an involuntary step away from him. 'He wants to meet *me*!' she echoed disbelievingly. 'Are you sure?'

'Por supuesto.' Enrique gave a shrug. 'You are David's mother. It is more than time for him to acknowledge your connection to this family.'

Cassandra moved her head from side to side. 'You did this,' she said accusingly. 'You persuaded him to meet me.' She twisted her hands together. 'Did you ever consider my feelings? What if I don't want to meet him?'

Enrique stared at her. 'You would defy him? Knowing that his health is far from good?'

'That's blackmail!'

'No.' Enrique was patient. 'It is—how do you say it?—common sense, no? I thought you would be glad to hear that my father has accepted the situation. It was not easy for me, breaking such news to him.'

Cassandra's breathing felt as if it had been suspended. 'You've told him David is your son?'

'Yes.' Enrique made a dismissive movement with his shoulders. 'But David himself does not know yet. I thought you would prefer it if I did not tell him.'

'You got that right.' Cassandra felt as if her life was moving out of control. 'I—then it's David he wants to see,' she added. 'Why don't you admit it? Julio de Montoya does not want to meet me.'

'He does,' insisted Enrique inflexibly. He paused and then added reluctantly, 'He has already met David. The boy was eager to meet his grandfather,' he continued, before she could make any objection. 'He saw the car arrive and he came to meet us.'

He would, thought Cassandra tightly. So that was where David had been all afternoon. It hurt a little that her son hadn't bothered to ask her permission. But, since coming to Tuarega, David had become a stranger to her in some ways.

'So where is he now?' she asked, and Enrique expelled a weary sigh.

'He is with my father,' he said flatly. And then, 'Why do I get the feeling that you are going to blame me for what David has done?'

'Who else can I blame?' she demanded, not altogether fairly. 'If you'd never come to find us, we wouldn't be having this conversation now.'

Enrique stiffened, his eyes dark and guarded. 'Are you saying you would have preferred it if we'd never met again?'

'Yes! *No!* Oh, I don't know.' Cassandra cupped her hot cheeks in confusion. 'You'd better leave me.' And as he arched an enquiring brow, she indicated her tee shirt and shorts. 'I can't meet your father dressed like this.'

'Cassandra—'

His anguished use of her name was almost her undoing. It

would have been so easy to give in to his persuasive tongue and let him bear the burden of what came after. But she had the awful feeling that Enrique still had his own agenda. She feared that without the knowledge that David was his son, and not Antonio's, he would never have attempted to rekindle emotions that had surely been deeply buried in the past.

CHAPTER FOURTEEN

'So when is David coming home?'

Henry Skyler, Cassandra's employer at the bookstore, was nothing if not direct and she gave him a determined smile. 'At the end of the summer holidays,' she replied brightly, as if there wasn't a shred of doubt in her mind. 'Do you want me to get rid of this dump bin? We don't have enough copies to fill it any more.'

'Oh, yes.' Henry nodded. 'That thriller did sell rather well, didn't it? People seem to have an insatiable appetite for that kind of book.' He rubbed his hands together. 'Good for business, of course.'

Cassandra nodded and started taking the few copies of the book that were left from the stand, waiting for Henry to return to his office at the back of the shop. But he remained where he was.

'You must miss him,' he said, returning to his earlier topic, and Cassandra's teeth ground together in frustration. 'I don't think I could have abandoned my son with strangers for—what?—three months?'

'Ten weeks, actually,' Cassandra corrected him shortly, but it was a moot point. Counting the two weeks they had been on holiday, David would have been away nearly three months by the time he came home. *If* he came home, she amended tensely. There were no guarantees in the arrangement. So far, she had had one phone call from David, and that was a couple of weeks ago now. Since then, she had heard nothing.

'All the same—'

'Henry, they're not strangers! They're his family!' she protested, desperately wanting to avoid a discussion about the situation. 'Where do you want me to put these books? Shall I stack them with the new fiction or put them back on the shelf?'

'With the new fiction, I think,' said Henry absently, obviously more interested in David's whereabouts than in that of his stock. 'And you say you don't mind? Aren't you afraid David won't want to come home?'

Cassandra heaved a sigh. 'Look, David wanted to stay,' she said tightly. 'His grandfather had just come home from hospital and they needed time to get to know one another. The hardest part was getting his school to agree to giving him the last few weeks of term off.'

Liar!

Cassandra was amazed she could make such a statement without her tongue falling out. God! Contacting the educational authorities and arranging for David to miss school for several weeks had been the least of her worries. Returning home to Luton airport without him: that had been the hard part.

'Well, if you say so,' said Henry now, realising he wasn't going to persuade her to part with any juicy gossip about her in-laws. He grimaced. 'He's a lucky boy. I wish I could discover I had a wealthy Spanish grandfather.'

Cassandra forced another smile and to her relief Henry left her to get on with her work. But she doubted if it would be the last she'd hear of it. He was intensely inquisitive, and learning that they'd accidentally encountered her late husband's family while they were in Spain had certainly aroused his interest. And his suspicions, she conceded ruefully. Even to her ears, it had sounded an unlikely scenario.

But she had no intention of telling him about David's hand in it. As far as Henry was concerned, her son had been as surprised to meet his mother's in-laws as she had, and she intended it to stay that way.

A customer came in as she was stacking the books, and she was glad of the diversion to take her thoughts from her son. She tried not to think about what he was doing or who he was with too often. Or acknowledge the uneasy belief that she might have made a terrible mistake in allowing David to stay with his father.

Yet, after the customer had departed, she wondered for the

umpteenth time what she could have done differently. If she'd insisted on David coming home with her, he'd have been miserable. Besides, it would only have been a matter of time before either Enrique or his father got the European courts involved and obtained a court order allowing the boy to spend time with his Spanish family. And what kind of a future would that have portended for any of them?

No, she had had no choice but to agree to Julio de Montoya's request. Anything else would have created even more bitterness between them, and for her son's sake she had had to swallow her pride. But, oh, it had been a painful decision, and even now she wondered how Julio had persuaded her to do it.

When she'd arrived at her father-in-law's suite of rooms that afternoon nearly three weeks ago, she didn't know what she'd expected of him. Anger, of course; hostility, definitely. However delighted he might have been to learn he had a grandson, she'd been certain that Enrique had exaggerated his father's desire to meet her. To *berate* her, perhaps. To deliver the kind of tirade Enrique had bestowed on the unfortunate Consuela; she'd been prepared for that. What she hadn't been prepared for was Julio's cordiality; his reasonableness; his apparent willingness to accept that she'd had good reasons for keeping David's existence to herself.

Of course, when she'd first been shown into Julio's room, she'd known none of that. In his impressive sitting room, with its deep ochre-tinted walls and heavy furniture, she'd been confronted by all the members of his immediate family, and it had been incredibly daunting.

David had been there, of course, but she hadn't felt she could look to her son for any support. Of all of them, he had had the most to lose, financially at least, and where the de Montoyas were concerned, as she knew to her cost, financial considerations were paramount.

Elena de Montoya had been standing beside her husband's wheelchair. Slim and autocratic, her expression had, as always, been impossible to read, though Cassandra had sensed that she didn't altogether approve of her husband dealing with something so potentially explosive on his first day home.

Enrique had been there, too, she remembered. He had been lounging against the wrought iron grille that framed the windows, his dark eyes narrowed and intent. The rich red curtains had accentuated his sombre countenance, and she had made a determined effort not to look his way.

Julio, himself, had proved to be a mere shadow of the man Cassandra remembered. At Antonio's funeral service, he had appeared so strong, so powerful; a dominant figure whom she had marvelled that Antonio had dared to oppose. But now he was older, frailer, showing the effects of the heart surgery Enrique had told her about. And infinitely less intimidating.

'Cassandra.' Julio had said her name slowly and succinctly, his accent, like his son's, giving her name a foreign sibilance. 'Thank you for coming.'

Cassandra could have said that she hadn't had much choice, but she didn't. Instead, she moved her shoulders in a dismissive gesture, saying politely, 'I hope you're feeling better, *señor*.'

'I have been better,' he agreed, using her term. 'But the news my son has given me has gone a long way towards advancing my recovery.' He held up a veined hand, summoning David to approach him. 'This boy is my passport to health, Cassandra. My hope for the future.' He took David's hand between both of his. '*Sí, hijo?* You agree, do you not?'

David's smile came and went, the look he cast towards his mother mirroring his uncertainty. Cassandra realised that he was still unsure of her reaction, and she was so eager to reassure her son that she inadvertently gave him the go-ahead to say whatever he liked.

'I'm sure he does,' she blurted swiftly, surprising all of them, and David wasted no time in assuring his grandfather that he loved being here at Tuarega.

There was more of the same, with Elena joining in to tell her husband that David was already beginning to speak a little Spanish, which was news to Cassandra. Still, it pleased the old man, and if it wasn't for Enrique, a disturbing presence beside the windows, she might believe that some kind of compromise was possible.

But then, once again, Julio did the unexpected. With infinite courtesy, but with an unmistakable edge of steel in his voice, he asked his wife, his son, and his grandson to leave them. He wanted to speak to his daughter-in-law alone, he said, by way of an explanation. There were misunderstandings between them, long-standing grievances that needed to be cleared up before they could embark on a lasting relationship. He said he hoped they would all understand and give him and Cassandra some breathing space.

Elena protested, saying that he wasn't well enough to conduct any kind of healing process now, but he was adamant, and it was left to Enrique to voice the loudest objections.

'I think I should stay,' he said, which was the first remark he'd made since Cassandra came into the room. And, although his father blustered, Cassandra knew that Julio would be no match for his son.

'I'd prefer it if you left,' she declared then, aware that she might be being a little foolhardy, but persisting with it anyway. She had no desire for Enrique to fight her battles for her. 'I'd like to hear what your father has to say.'

Enrique looked as if he would like to argue with her. The glitter in his eyes was intimidating and promised a certain retribution. But he accepted their decision. With studied deliberation, he left the room with his mother and his son, his only protest the grazing brush of his thumb against Cassandra's bare arm as he passed.

Cassandra shivered now, remembering his touch with every fibre of her being. She hadn't known then that that was the last time Enrique would want to touch her; hadn't comprehended that he'd known exactly what his father was going to say to her.

Julio had been tired. She'd known that. Despite his assertion to the contrary, the day had exhausted him, and Cassandra had wondered since if his choice of time had been deliberate; if he'd known exactly how she would feel, confronted by a man in his condition.

Whatever, at that moment she'd been preparing herself for the kind of reception she'd expected when she'd first entered his rooms, and she'd been taken aback when he'd invited her to sit in the chair nearest to him and asked if she'd like some refreshment.

She'd refused, of course. She'd wanted to get this over with, for him to make his feelings known and allow her to return to the anonymity of her rooms. But now that they were alone, Julio had been in no hurry to get to the point. He'd asked about her father, about her family, assuring himself that they were well before going on to ask about David, about where he went to school, about the life they shared back in England.

Cassandra had been disarmed; she recognised that now. She'd been expecting censure, criticism, and what she'd got had been tolerance and kindness, and an obvious desire to put her at her ease.

'Enrique has told me the whole story,' Julio said at last, when Cassandra was totally at his mercy. 'He is not proud of his part in it. He bitterly regrets being the cause of this estrangement between our families, and it is his wish that you allow us to take some of the strain of raising the boy from now on.'

Cassandra was taken aback. It was news to her that Enrique considered his actions the reason for her cutting herself and David off from the de Montoyas, but who was she to argue with his father? Surely he must know his son better than she did.

Then, before she could express any protest, he went on to ask how she'd feel if he requested that she allow David to stay in Spain for a few more weeks instead of accompanying her home at the end of her holiday. He said he was sure David would take her lead in this, and, although she doubted that premise, she was hard-pressed to find a reason to refuse. When he went on to suggest that he might not get such an opportunity again, Cassandra knew she couldn't say no. Julio's tacit reference to his own mortality was a powerful lever, and David would never forgive her if she denied him possibly his only chance to get to know his Spanish grandfather.

The one condition she insisted on was that David remained in ignorance of his real father's identity. She said she understood their eagerness to integrate him into their family, but she would prefer to wait until he was older before burdening him with that news. She just hoped that when that time came, David would forgive her. As far as she was concerned, he was the innocent victim here.

She slept badly again that night and awoke to the news that, once again, Enrique had left the *palacio*. According to David, who seemed enviably well informed about these things, he'd gone to Cadiz to attend to business matters for his father and wouldn't be back until the following day at the earliest.

To Cassandra, who'd half expected Enrique to come and see her the night before, it was the last straw. It seemed that everything Enrique had done had been to an end, and now that she'd agreed to allow David to stay at Tuarega he had nothing more to gain. He hadn't even had the decency to thank her for her co-operation. She fretted throughout the next seventy-two hours, before deciding to try for an earlier flight home. There was nothing for her here, and she guessed that everyone would feel infinitely happier when she was gone.

David objected, of course. Even though she explained that, since speaking to his English grandfather, she'd been worried about the situation back home, her son wanted her to stay until Enrique got back.

'I'm sure he'll expect you to stay,' he insisted, but Cassandra was equally insistent that he wouldn't.

'I told you,' she assured him gently, 'Enrique and I have nothing in common.' *Except you!* 'He'll be glad not to have to worry about me any more.' *If he ever had!*

She flew back to England the following day, having been driven to the airport in Seville by Julio's chauffeur. She didn't see the old man again, though Elena had the courtesy to come out to bid her farewell.

'We will look after David,' she said, a possessive hand resting on the boy's shoulder, and Cassandra found it incredibly difficult not to snatch her son into her arms and take him with her.

She sighed now, realising that she was wasting time fretting about something over which she had no real control. She'd committed herself to allowing the de Montoyas to play a part in her son's life and if her father thought she was mad: well, so be it.

It was a week later, and Cassandra was serving a group of teenagers who were looking for copies of Virgil's *Aeneid*, when her eyes were drawn to the sight of a gleaming limousine drawing up outside the shop. It wasn't usual for cars to stop outside The Bookworm, and she could only assume that whoever was driving was a stranger to the district.

A stranger!

Her mouth went dry, and she inadvertently gave one of the youths a ten-pound note instead of a five in change. My God, what if it's Enrique? she thought unsteadily. What was he likely to be doing there?

Fortunately, her youthful customer was honest, but her nervous laugh brought Henry to the front of the shop to see what was going on. 'I'm just trying to cut your profits,' she managed lightly as the teenagers left the shop, but her face was burning and she soon realised that Henry wasn't listening to her in any case.

'Nice car,' he remarked instead, as the limousine idled at the kerb. 'But he'll get a parking ticket if he stays there.'

'Hmm.' Cassandra told herself she didn't care what happened to the limousine. It wasn't going to be Enrique. If he'd cared anything about her, he'd never have stayed away as he had. And, so long as it didn't belong to any other de Montoya, she had nothing to worry about. 'Um—is it all right if I go for my lunch now?'

'What?' Henry looked blankly at her. Then, without answering her question, 'Hey, someone's getting out of the car.'

'Henry!' Cassandra tried not to look towards the window. 'Don't be so nosy.' She paused. 'About lunch—'

'My God, he's coming in,' Henry interrupted her quickly. 'He looks foreign, Cass. Are you sure you don't know who it is?'

Cassandra's head jerked up, a mixture of fear and excitement churning in her stomach. Henry was right. A darkly tanned individual was entering the bookstore. But it wasn't Enrique, as she'd imagined; *as she'd hoped*? Nor was it his father. But the man was known to her. It was the chauffeur who had driven her to the airport when she left.

'*Señora*,' he said, making directly for Cassandra, and Henry's eyes widened as he looked at his assistant. '*Por favor, señora*, Senor de Montoya wishes to speak with you.'

Cassandra quivered. The man—she knew his name was Salvador—was waiting for her response, but she was too shocked to answer him.

'*Señora?*' echoed Henry admiringly, making a wry face, and Cassandra struggled to pull herself together.

'Señor de Montoya?' she got out at last, hardly daring to voice the words. 'Señor Enrique de—'

'Señor Julio, *señora*,' Salvador interrupted her swiftly, nodding towards the car behind him. 'He is waiting, *señora*. You will come, *si*?'

Julio!

Cassandra felt sick. For a moment she'd allowed herself the luxury of believing that Enrique hadn't abandoned her, that he cared about her and not about what he wanted from her. But now he had his son! The child he'd never known he had. He didn't need her any more.

Besides, she should have had more sense, she chided herself. A man who'd apparently allowed his father to do what he should have done himself was hardly likely to be having second thoughts now.

And, as her head cleared, she thought she could guess why Julio de Montoya was here. They had given her three weeks to get used to being without David, and now it was time to put the second part of their plan into operation. Julio was going to suggest that her son was happy with them, that they could give him so much more than she could, that perhaps she might consider allowing him to live with them instead of returning him to England at the end of the summer.

No!

'Yes, go along, Cass,' urged Henry, evidently eager to find out what they wanted for himself. 'It is lunch time. I can spare you for—well, for a couple of hours.'

A couple of hours! Cassandra's lips twisted. Usually, she had a struggle to get half an hour in the middle of the day.

'I—I don't know—'

She was shaking her head, wondering how on earth she was going to avoid talking to Julio de Montoya, when another voice spoke from the doorway.

'Cassandra!' It was Julio himself, still pale and drawn, but evidently much recovered from the last time she'd seen him. Even his voice had acquired a little of the imperiousness she remembered from ten years ago. 'Please,' he added, with surprising humility. 'We need to talk.'

'Do we?' She was uneasy, but there was really no contest.

'I believe so,' he asserted heavily, and now she saw that he was leaning on an ebony cane. 'Will you come?'

Henry watched from the doorway as Salvador assisted first his employer and then Cassandra into the back of the limousine. Julio apologised for preceding her, but it had become apparent that he was still far from strong. Cassandra was amazed that Señora de Montoya had allowed her husband to make the journey himself.

But perhaps he'd insisted that his powers of persuasion were superior to hers and those of his son. There was no doubt that he had succeeded before, and the fact that Enrique wasn't with him seemed to point to the fact that he had decided to leave it to his father. Again.

For her part, Cassandra was too tense to worry about protocol. Taking her seat beside Julio in the back of the car, all she could think about was David and how bleak her future would be if he didn't want to come home.

'*Por favor, Salvador,*' said Julio once she was seated, indicating that the chauffeur should drive on, and Cassandra glanced behind her to see Henry turning rather disappointedly back into the shop.

'Your employer?' asked Enrique's father as she swung round again, and she nodded.

'Henry Skyler,' she conceded. 'It's his shop.'

Julio inclined his head. 'You have worked there long?'

'Several years,' she agreed, her tone sharpening. She wished he would tell her why he was here and stop wasting time. They had nothing in common and pretending he was interested in her life was just a way to get her to let down her guard. 'Where are we going?'

'Ah.' Julio appeared to acknowledge her impatience. 'If you will permit, we will go to the hotel where I usually stay when I am in London.'

Cassandra pressed her lips together. So, it was to be a prolonged encounter. Instead of tea and sympathy, it was to be lunch and sympathy. Whatever way you looked at it, she doubted it was her feelings he was thinking about.

'Is this necessary?' she asked, deciding she would rather know the worst right away. 'I realise you might find it easier to say what you have to say in a restaurant, where I'd be constrained to be polite, but I'd rather you were honest with me.'

'Honest with you, Cassandra?' To her surprise, Julio looked disturbed now. 'You would rather I came right out and told you what has happened *en seguida*? At once? *Que?* You have reason to believe I bring bad news?'

Cassandra swallowed. 'Well, don't you?'

Julio stared at her with troubled eyes. 'Elena,' he said with sudden comprehension. 'Elena has telephoned you. She promised she would not, but I should have known—'

'Señora de Montoya hasn't contacted me,' Cassandra interrupted him shortly. 'But it's obvious you're not here to ask after my health. We don't have that kind of a relationship.'

'No.' Julio conceded the point. 'And you are sure my wife has not been in touch with you? That she hasn't warned you—?'

'Warned me?' Cassandra looked at him. 'Warned me of what? That I shouldn't upset you when you tell me you want to keep David in Spain? That I should just accept the fact that you intend to appropriate my son?'

'Your son?' Julio looked dismayed. 'You think this is about David?'

'Well, isn't it?'

Cassandra wouldn't allow the sudden curl of fear to daunt her. Why else would Julio de Montoya have made this journey? Only something terribly important to him would have persuaded him to come and see her only weeks after such a serious operation. And, aside from his grandson, what else could it be?

His son?

The thought caught Cassandra unawares, although she suspected that that was what she had been suppressing since Enrique's father had denied this was anything to do with David. A feeling of coldness enveloped her. Oh, God, what could possibly have happened to cause this arrogant old autocrat to come to her?

'I—it has to be David,' she insisted, refusing to let him see what she was thinking. 'What else could it be?'

Julio shook his head. 'I—I would prefer it if you could wait until we reach the hotel,' he said stiffly, glancing towards Salvador, and she realised it was against his principles to discuss family matters in front of the chauffeur.

But Cassandra was in no mood to humour him. 'Is it David?' she persisted, still refusing to believe that it could be anything else. 'You might as well tell me. I think I deserve a little time to prepare my defence.'

'Your defence?' Julio was ironic. 'Oh, Cassandra, you are so cold; so suspicious. Does it not occur to you that if I wanted to—what was it you said? Appropriate your son? Yes, that was the term you used—appropriate your son, I would have allowed my lawyer to deal with it?'

'Then—'

'There has been an accident,' said Julio heavily, and not without some reluctance. 'As you insist on—'

'An accident?' Cassandra interrupted him again, her heart in her mouth. 'David?'

'No, Enrique,' said the old man wearily. 'My son. My only son. I have come to beg you to return to Spain with me. If you do not, I fear—I fear the consequences.'

CHAPTER FIFTEEN

APPROACHING Tuarega from the north was different from approaching it from the south. The north was wilder, harsher, the landscape punctuated by dry riverbeds and rocky ravines where prickly pear and spiky agave were the only vegetation.

Sitting in the back of another limousine, Cassandra paid little attention to her surroundings. Darkness had fallen, and it was difficult to think of anything except the reason why she was here. The stark peaks of the *sierra*, briefly glimpsed in the headlights of the car, only accentuated her feelings of isolation, of being far from everything she knew, everything she believed. She still wasn't absolutely convinced that she should have come, and she didn't know if she could take another rejection.

Nonetheless, she had thought of little but Enrique since Julio had delivered the news of his accident. Hearing how he had entered one of the pens where a rogue bull was corralled and been gored for his pains had horrified her. It seemed so unlike him, somehow. David had told her that Enrique had always cautioned him to show great respect for the animals, and, according to Julio, Juan had warned him not to approach the beast.

So why had he? Julio's opinion was that his son had had something on his mind; that he hadn't been thinking when he'd entered the pen and found himself face-to-face with an enraged bull. Whatever, before any of the hands could create a diversion, the animal had charged, its sharp horns ripping Enrique's arm and gouging an ugly gash in his thigh.

Cassandra shivered now, just thinking of it. Flesh wounds always bled profusely and Julio had admitted that the floor of the pen had been soaked with his son's blood. It had taken four men to drag the infuriated beast away from him and, since then, the bull had been destroyed.

Enrique had been unconscious when a helicopter had air-lifted him to the hospital in Seville where his father had so recently been a patient. He'd needed a blood transfusion, but fortunately the wound in his leg had just missed the artery. Even so, he'd lost a lot of blood, and for several days his condition had been closely monitored.

Cassandra found it incredible that all this could have been going on while she had been totally ignorant of it. No one had phoned her; no one had told her that the man she was very much afraid she had never stopped loving was fighting for his life. Only now had she been apprised of the situation. Only now had the de Montoyas been forced to humble themselves and contact her. And that only because although Enrique's physical condition was much improved, his mental state was proving a cause for concern.

'He seems—uninterested in everything,' Julio had told her, with evident frustration. 'The accident happened—what? Two weeks ago? At least that. And his wounds are healing well. After all, they are used to such injuries in my country. You English think the bull is such a helpless creature, but I have seen men lose limbs—lose their very lives—in the cause of the *corrida*.'

Cassandra hadn't answered that. The fact was that in the *corrida* the bull was always fighting for its life. But that was their culture. It wasn't up to her to criticise something she really knew nothing about.

'He should be up and about by now,' Julio had continued unhappily. 'He has duties; responsibilities. He knows I am not capable of doing very much and yet he will not listen to me, will not talk to me, will not even talk to David.'

So why did they think he would talk to her? Cassandra wondered uneasily. Julio hadn't offered an explanation. He hadn't even mentioned David's reaction to all this, merely responding to her enquiry by saying the boy was with his grandmother and leaving it at that.

Yet surely Enrique would want to spend time with his son?

But when she'd mentioned as much to Julio, he'd been curiously reticent. 'He sees no one,' he'd insisted shortly and with evident reluctance. 'Apart from Carlos Mendoza, *por su-puesto*. You will see for yourself, if you will come.'

As if she'd had any choice, thought Cassandra now, taut with apprehension and anxiety. What if Enrique refused to see her? What then? Would they pack her off back to England again? She doubted they'd have any choice. And, God knew, she wouldn't want to stay in those circumstances...

The limousine was descending into a valley now and, although Cassandra had no real knowledge of where they were, she sensed they were nearing their destination. She could see lamps burning at the gates of a building ahead of them and, below, the clustered lights of a small village. She guessed they were still some distance from Tuarega itself, but perhaps this might be an appropriate time to warn Julio of their imminent arrival.

The old man had dozed on and off for most of their journey and she wasn't surprised. She guessed he was exhausted. This had been a gruelling day for a man in his condition, and she was amazed at his stamina.

She certainly hadn't expected him to suggest that they left for Spain that afternoon. They'd had lunch at his hotel, but, after gaining her consent to his request for her to return to Spain with him, he'd been anxious to get away.

He'd had a private jet waiting for them at Stanstead Airport. Cassandra had only had time to phone her father and give him the briefest of explanations, asking him to relay the news to Henry Skyler, before leaving.

But, before she could do anything, she realised the big car was slowing and Julio opened his eyes as they turned between the stone gateposts she'd glimpsed earlier. Ahead of them, she could see the dark stone walls of a strange building, and her stomach prickled with nerves. What now? she wondered apprehensively. Where were they? Why had Julio brought her here?

He was struggling to sit up now. He had slumped against the squabs since they left Seville, but now he endeavoured to straighten his stiff spine and bring some feeling back into his cramped limbs.

Then he caught Cassandra looking at him, and his dark eyes widened in obvious enquiry. 'Is something wrong?'

'Where are we?' she demanded, aware of the tremor in her voice. 'This isn't Tuarega.'

'*Bien*, it is Tuarega land,' replied Julio, with a lift of his shoulders. 'I thought I told you. Enrique has been—how do you say it?—covered up here at La Hacienda since he came home from the hospital, no? He does not care for any company.'

Cassandra blinked. 'Covered up?' she echoed blankly. Then comprehension dawned. 'Oh, you mean—*holed* up,' she corrected him tensely. Then, glancing up at the forbidding aspect of the dwelling, 'You mean, this is Enrique's house?'

'La Hacienda,' he agreed, a little impatiently. 'With your permission, I will bid you farewell here.'

'What?' Cassandra stared at him. 'You're leaving me here? Alone?'

'You will not be alone,' replied Julio implacably. 'Enrique is here. And Mendoza. Mendoza will see that you have everything you need.'

'But—'

'Cassandra, I am depending on you to save my son's sanity. Believe me, I would not have asked for your help unless— unless there was no other alternative.'

Unless he was desperate, thought Cassandra bitterly. Could he have made it any plainer? She was only here because everything—and everyone—else had failed.

The car had stopped and now a door opened and a shaft of light fell across the bonnet of the limousine. Carlos Mendoza stood in the doorway, clearly expecting them. Like his employer's, his face bore an expression of concern, and Cassandra only paused to cast another doubtful look at Julio before accepting Salvador's hand to help her out of the car.

Carlos came down the steps. '*Bienvenido a La Hacienda, señora,*' he said, his smile warm and sincere. 'Do you have a bag?'

'No bags, Carlos,' replied Cassandra ruefully, turning back to look at the car. '*Adiós, señor.*'

'*Hasta mañana, Cassandra,*' responded Julio de Montoya, leaning out of the limousine. 'Until tomorrow.'

Salvador slammed the car door and went around to take his seat behind the wheel, and Cassandra waited until the vehicle had started to move away before looking again at the house. She was feeling weak and inadequate, and she had no idea why Enrique's father thought she might have more success with his son than he had.

'*Es por aquí, señora,*' said Carlos gently, urging her up the steps and into the building. 'This way.' He paused to close the heavy door behind them. 'You had a good journey, no?'

Cassandra shook her head. 'I suppose so,' she said, looking about her a little dazedly. They were in a marble-floored entry, where a curving staircase with a wrought-iron banister wound to the upper floors of the house. Beside the staircase, long mirrors hung opposite one another, and a huge bowl of purple orchids was reflected over and over again in their lamplit depths. 'I—where is Enrique?'

'You wish to eat, *señora*?' asked Carlos, without answering her. 'Maria—she has left you a small—um—*comida, sí*?'

'Maria?'

Cassandra looked at him and he spread his hands. 'Maria is—*la criada, señora,*' he replied awkwardly, and she frowned.

'The—the maid?' she ventured at last, trying to remember the little Spanish she had learned and he nodded in some relief.

'*Sí*, the maid, *señora.*' He paused, gesturing through an archway beyond the curve of the staircase. '*Por aquí.*'

Cassandra hesitated. Then, 'Enrique,' she said firmly, having no interest in the food he was offering. 'I'd like to see him first.'

'*Señora*—'

Carlos spoke guardedly, his diffidence revealing a wealth of uncertainty. Cassandra guessed that, although he had been forced to accept Julio's decision to bring her here, he was by no means convinced of its wisdom.

But, before he could say any more, someone else interrupted them. 'Why?' enquired a voice that was both unbearably cold and undeniably familiar and Cassandra lifted her head to find Enrique standing looking down at them from the head of the first flight of stairs.

Cassandra's lips parted in dismay. This was not the way she'd hoped to announce her arrival. It was obvious from the hostility in Enrique's tone that he had known nothing of his father's meddling, and her mouth dried at the realisation that he could just turn around and refuse to speak to her.

And he needed to speak to someone, she thought worriedly. Whatever his motives, Julio hadn't exaggerated his fears for his son's well-being. Enrique looked grey; emaciated. In three short weeks his skin had lost the glow of health, and his loss of weight was evident in the cream knit sweater and drawstring sweats that hung on his lean frame.

'I—how are you?' she got out awkwardly, trying desperately not to show how concerned she was.

Enrique's lips compressed into a thin line. 'What are you doing here, Cassandra?' he asked at last, his long fingers curling and uncurling about the iron balustrade. 'How did you get here? Who told you where I was?'

'Does it matter?' Cassandra caught her lower lip between her teeth and glanced briefly at Carlos. Then, returning her attention to the man at the head of the stairs, 'Um—can we talk?'

'Oh, please!' Enrique's tone was sardonic now. 'I do not think you and I have anything to talk about.' He paused. 'I imagine it must have been my father who brought you here.' His lips twisted. 'I did not realise he was that desperate.'

Cassandra winced at the deliberate insult, but she stood her ground. 'Yes,' she said, looking up at him. 'Your father did bring me here. But if I hadn't wanted to come, I wouldn't have accepted his invitation.'

'How sweet!'

Enrique's voice was cold and Carlos evidently decided that his presence was superfluous. 'If you will excuse me, *señor*,' he murmured, and Enrique made an indifferent gesture of affirmation. The man bowed and disappeared through a door at the end of the hall and Cassandra was left with the unpleasant feeling that Carlos knew she was wasting her time.

'Enrique—' she began again, but before she could say any more he interrupted her.

'No,' he said bleakly. 'We have nothing to say to one another. I do not know what tale my father concocted to persuade you to return to Tuarega, but, whatever it was, he obviously exaggerated. As you can see, I am still—what is it you say?— in one piece, *sí*?'

'Are you?' Cassandra's fingers felt sticky where they were gripping the strap of her haversack. She hesitated. 'I know you've been ill.'

Enrique scowled. 'I am sure you do. My father would use anything to gain his own ends.' He suddenly looked unbearably weary. 'Go away, Cassandra. I do not have the inclination to speak with you now.'

Or the strength, thought Cassandra anxiously, her spirits plummeting when he turned and walked away, out of her sight. Dear God, no wonder Julio was desperate. He must despair of finding any way to reach his son. The amazing thing was that he thought *she* might.

Cassandra set her haversack down on the hall table and looked doubtfully about her. To her right was the room Carlos had indicated where the maid had left her something to eat. But she wasn't hungry. She could always go in search of Carlos, of course. He was probably close at hand, waiting for some sign from her that she either wanted to be taken to Tuarega or back to the airport in Seville. But she couldn't leave. However unlikely, Julio believed she might have a chance of getting through to Enrique. She had to try.

Taking a deep breath, she put her hand on the banister and started up the stairs. Subtle lights set into the ceiling illuminated her way and a broad-based standard lamp occupied a prominent position on the first landing. The stairs continued up to a second floor, but Cassandra knew Enrique hadn't continued upward. He'd crossed the landing and disappeared into one of the twin corridors that confronted her, and, after a moment's hesitation, she took the one to her left.

Here the illumination came from a string of spotlights that highlighted the paintings that adorned the walls. Not gloomy paintings, like she'd seen at Tuarega, but more modern renditions of local scenes, one of which bore a strong resemblance to Tuarega itself.

But Cassandra knew she was only distracting herself by looking at the paintings, that sooner or later she would have to confront her own inadequacies. She was intensely conscious of the sound of her thick-soled boots squeaking on the tiled floor, aware that the ankle-length cotton skirt and tee shirt she'd worn for work that morning were totally unsuitable in these elegant surroundings. She should have insisted on going home to change, she thought pointlessly. But she had allowed Julio to infect her with his concern for his son's recovery.

At the end of the corridor, double doors stood open onto a dimly lit vestibule. Nervously, she stepped across a circular rug, whose vivid colours were muted in the shadowy light, and paused at the entrance to a large sitting room. Pale walls hung with hand-sewn tapestries; overstuffed beige sofas and leather chairs flanking a cream stone fireplace; and cushions everywhere: on the sofas, on the chairs, and in some cases piled in heaps upon the huge fringed rug. It was the cushions that gave the room its colour, its warm ambience, its attractive personality.

But it was the man standing on the balcony beyond open floor-length windows who drew Cassandra's eyes. Like the stairwell, this room was lit by a handful of lamps, but the open windows allowed a glimpse of the starlit sky outside. And of the moon, a sickle of white against that night-dark canopy.

Enrique hadn't seen her. As far as he knew, she was still downstairs, possibly even preparing to leave, and she wondered if the balcony overlooked the entry. But that was wishful thinking, she thought ruefully. And besides, if Enrique was looking for her to leave, it was not because he was hoping she would stay.

She didn't know what to do; what to say. Even coming into his suite of rooms was an unwarranted liberty. He hadn't invited her there. In fact, he'd made it blatantly obvious that she wasn't welcome here. So why didn't she just accept defeat and leave?

Because she couldn't.

Because, no matter how painful this might be for her, she had to try and talk to him. To talk some sense into him, she reflected dubiously. If his depression had something to do with David, to do with the fact that she had kept his existence a secret from him all these years, she had to try and do something about it. Even if it meant leaving David here longer than the limited number of weeks she had agreed to.

Or was that being absurdly ingenuous? What if this was all a clever ploy instigated by Enrique and his father to gain control of her son? She was certainly easily persuaded if that was so.

But she dismissed the idea as soon as it generated itself. This was no ploy, no plan of Julio's to delude her into giving her son away. Enrique looked ill; far more ill than she had expected. How serious had his injuries been, for God's sake? And was there any chance that he'd confide in her?

'Hasta nunca, Carlos.'

While she'd been hovering just inside the door, trying to decide what she could say to attract his attention, Enrique had apparently heard something and assumed it was the manservant. And, realising she would have to identify herself, she found the words to say.

'Hasta nunca?' she echoed softly. 'What does that mean?'

Enrique swung round, swaying a little as he did so, and she longed to go and put her arms around him. 'It means, get lost,' he informed her harshly. 'And it applies to you just as much as to Carlos.'

Cassandra blew out a breath. 'That's not very polite. I always thought Spaniards prided themselves on being excessively polite. Although I suppose your family is a law unto itself.'

Enrique's eyes were hooded, so she couldn't read their expression, but his nostrils flared. 'As you say,' he conceded, after a moment. 'Will you go now?'

Cassandra shook her head. 'I can't.'

'Why not? Carlos will call Salvador for you, if you wish. Or a cab, if you would prefer. We do have telephones at La Hacienda.'

'Enrique—'

He breathed a deep sigh and, leaving the balcony rail, he walked wearily back into the sitting room. 'You are determined to persist with this, are you not?' he said heavily. 'Why? Why are you here? Of what possible interest can it be to you that I have had a minor accident that resulted in a short spell in hospital?'

'It was hardly a minor accident,' exclaimed Cassandra at once, and he shook his head.

'*Sí*, it was.' He rolled back the sleeve of his sweater, exposing a raw scar on his forearm. '*Aquí tiene*, it is healing. Juan has had many such injuries over the years and his family do not panic at the first sight of blood.'

Cassandra felt sick, her stomach twisting at the thought of the pain he must have suffered before the paramedics could get to him. 'That—that wasn't your only injury,' she protested. 'I know you had to have a blood transfusion.'

'*Dios!*' Enrique propped himself against one of the sofas and Cassandra had the feeling he was in danger of falling without that support. 'I do not intend to show you my other injury, Cassandra.' He snorted. '*El viejo*—the old man—he has certainly laid a—how is it?—a guilt trip on you, no?'

'No.' She couldn't help moving a little closer even though he stiffened when she did so. 'Oh, Enrique, I've been so worried about you.'

'*Que?*' His lips twisted. 'And this from the woman who ran away rather than face me after confessing her cruel little deception? You must be careful in future, Cassandra. Wine can loosen the sharpest tongue.'

'I didn't run away,' insisted Cassandra indignantly. She took a breath. 'That was you.'

'Me?' Enrique stared at her for a moment and then he shook his head. 'No, Cassandra, I do not run away. I admit that when you told me that I was David's father I was glad to have to go to Seville to bring my father home. I needed a little time to come to terms with what you had told me. I admitted that. But I did not run away.'

Cassandra quivered. 'What about ten years ago?' she countered, unable to prevent herself, and his face contorted with sudden loathing. But whether it was for himself or for her, she had no way of knowing.

'Ten years ago,' he echoed bitterly. 'Ah, you do not intend for me to forget that, do you, *querida*.' He used a term of endearment, but there was no affection in his tone. 'You asked me once what I said to Antonio, *si*? Would it surprise you to hear that I said nothing? Nothing.' He shook his head. 'I made a mistake, Cassandra. A terrible mistake, I admit it. And I have been paying for it ever since.'

'You don't mean that.'

Cassandra was confused, and he bent his head to run weary hands through his hair. His hair needed cutting, she noticed inconsequentially. It overlapped his collar at the back. Then, lifting his head, he speared her with a tormented stare.

'I do mean it,' he said. 'But I see I am only satisfying whatever twisted thread of your nature brought you here.' His voice was rough. 'If my father had not told you about the accident, you would not be here. What did he tell you? Did he imply I was at death's door? I can think of no other reason why you would agree to see me again.'

'I wanted to see you!' The words were torn from her. 'And you know very well why I went back to England. You might not have been present at the interview I had with your father, but you knew what he was going to say. You wanted David to stay here. It was what you'd wanted all along, even before you knew David was your son. How could I insist on taking him back to England when it might be your father's only chance to get to know his grandson? I'm not that heartless, Enrique. Besides—' she heaved a sigh '—it was what David wanted.'

'So why did you not stay, too?'

'Because I have a job,' exclaimed Cassandra at once. 'I can't just take time off when I feel like it.'

'But your holiday was not over,' retorted Enrique, pushing

himself away from the sofa. 'You left without even having the—the courtesy to tell me goodbye.'

'You weren't there,' exclaimed Cassandra defensively. 'I was told you'd gone to Cadiz, on business for your father. I waited. I did.' This as Enrique pulled a wry face. 'But day followed day and you didn't come back.'

Enrique studied her indignant face. 'I almost believe you.'

'Almost?' she caught her breath. 'It's the truth!'

'Then why did you tell David that you did not want to see me again? That your own father was more important than waiting around for me to come back?'

'I—didn't say that.' But she had said something like it. Something that had persuaded David to intercede on her behalf. With, apparently, disastrous consequences.

'I can see you are having second thoughts,' said Enrique bitterly. 'You did tell David you never wanted to see me again. Why deny it now?'

'Because it wasn't true,' blurted Cassandra impulsively. 'Dear God, Enrique, you can't possibly believe that. Not—not after I'd told you—'

'That David is my son? His tone was harsh. 'That not only had I seduced you but I had also condemned you to spend the last nine years caring for my child? Oh, yes, I can see that that would persuade you to stay.'

'It wasn't like that,' protested Cassandra huskily. 'Why do you think I told you as I did? I didn't have to. I *wanted* to.'

'To torture me?'

'No!' Cassandra stared into his dark tormented face for a long moment and then, coming to a decision, she stepped forward and, reaching up, brushed his lips with hers. 'That's—that's why,' she added, a little breathlessly. 'Do you believe me now?'

Enrique didn't touch her. 'I believe you'll regret your impulsiveness,' he declared roughly. 'And I am forced to accept that you have a conscience. But that is all.'

Cassandra shook her head. 'You're wrong.'

'Am I?' Enrique breathed deeply. 'So what are you saying?

That what happened between us ten years ago meant something to you?'

Cassandra hesitated. 'You know it did.'

'Do I?' But he had the grace to look away as he added in a low hoarse voice, 'Yet you went ahead and married my brother.'

Cassandra nodded. 'Yes.'

Enrique's face contorted. 'How could you?'

Cassandra closed her eyes for a moment. 'I tried to tell him I couldn't marry him,' she insisted dully. 'I did. But he didn't want to hear it. He said that if I let him down, it would shame him; that it would prove to you and to the rest of his family that I really had only wanted to marry him because of who he was.' She lifted her lids again, to find Enrique, watching her with bleak unforgiving eyes. 'It's the truth. Can't you try and understand how I was feeling? I was nineteen years old, Enrique. I was in a state of shock. You—you'd left. I didn't know what to do.'

'You must have hated me,' said Enrique harshly, but it wasn't a vindication and she shivered.

'You don't understand,' she said again. 'Antonio—Antonio loved me. And I cared for him, too. I didn't know I was already carrying the seed of your child. I just wanted to do what was right. I—I swore to myself that I'd make him a good wife, and—and I would have. But then the accident happened. It was an accident, you know? Nothing else. Antonio never knew about us. I suppose I'd hoped he never would. But not in that way. Never in that way.'

'And if we had met again?' suggested Enrique with bitter emphasis, and she turned away.

'I—I—I can't answer that,' she said brokenly, and, unable to take any more, she stumbled towards the door.

She didn't make it. Before she'd gone a dozen yards Enrique caught her, his hands closing about her upper arms from behind and preventing her from going any further. Although his hands were slick with sweat, proving how weak he was, and she could feel the unsteadiness in his body, he somehow managed to drag her back against his shaking frame. Then his head dipped to find the vulnerable curve of her neck and she felt the roughness of his jaw against her skin.

'*Lo siento,*' he groaned, his lips moving against her flesh. 'I'm sorry. *Lo siento mucho.*' I'm so sorry. 'Will you forgive me?'

Cassandra tipped her head back against his shoulder, her arms crossing her body to capture his hands with hers. 'There—there's nothing to forgive.'

'There is,' he contradicted her huskily, turning her in his arms to cradle her face between his palms. 'I have been such a fool; such an arrogant fool. I have no right to ask for explanations from you when my own behaviour has been so much less than admirable.'

'Oh, Enrique—'

Her eyes were shining with unshed tears, but he wouldn't let her reassure him. 'Let me speak,' he said, and she could feel the tremor of his body through his hands. 'I told you that ten years ago I made a terrible mistake. I did. But the mistake was not in making love with you.' His thumbs brushed her cheeks. 'The mistake was in letting you go.'

Cassandra stared up at him. 'Enrique…'

'It is true. That was what I meant when I said I had been paying for it ever since.' His lips twisted. 'Oh, I have tried to deny it. I have tried to forget and move on with my life, but it has not worked. I am still unmarried, and until I read David's letter I believed I would never get the chance to speak to you again.'

'Enrique…'

'No, listen to me, *querida*. I want to tell you how it was when I saw you in Punta del Lobo. Until then, I had held out some hope that you were not the reason why I have resisted all my father's efforts to find me a wife. But when I saw you, when I saw the fire in your eyes—' He took a shuddering breath. '*Dios*, Cassandra, you must have known how I felt.'

'No.' She shook her head. 'All I saw was the shock you got when you saw David.'

'Ah!' He lowered his head and rested his forehead against

hers. 'That was a shock, *sí*. And a source of some envy on my part.'

'Envy?'

'I thought David was Antonio's child,' he reminded her drily. 'I was selfish enough to resent the fact that he wasn't mine.'

Cassandra lifted her hands to his shoulders. 'He's yours,' she said simply. 'You know that now.'

'Yes, I do.' He paused. 'But when I returned from Cadiz and found you gone—' He turned unsteadily away, as if the emotions his words had generated were too much for him. 'I am sorry. I have got to sit down...'

'Oh, Enrique!'

With sudden understanding, Cassandra put her arm about his waist and guided him to the nearest sofa. Then, when he was seated, she came down beside him, close enough so that her hip and thigh and the whole side of her body was touching his.

'I am sorry,' he said again, when she lifted a hand to stroke his damp forehead. 'You must think I am useless.'

'Just suffering from a surfeit of emotion,' she told him gently, leaning closer and depositing a soft kiss on his mouth. 'Oh, Enrique, why didn't you tell me how you felt?'

'I intended to,' he said, his eyes dark with passion. He was feeling stronger now that he was off his feet, and the arm that came about her shoulders, holding her against his chest, was surprisingly firm. 'But when I got back from Cadiz, you had gone.'

'There are phones,' she reminded him, and he closed his eyes briefly, as if recalling his anguish.

'There are,' he agreed. 'But I regret to say I am a proud man and I preferred not to humiliate myself again.'

'Again?'

'*Por supuesto*. I could not believe that after speaking to you in the gallery, and when I came to your bedroom, you could have any doubts about the way I felt about you. And when I came back and David told me what you had said—' He shrugged. 'I hardly needed my father to tell me what a fool I was.'

Cassandra caught her breath. 'He told you that?'

'As good as.' He sighed. 'He told me he had tried to persuade you to stay until the end of your holiday but that you had been determined to leave.'

'But he didn't.'

'I know that now.' Enrique grimaced. 'I also realise that that was why he insisted I must attend to his affairs before addressing my own. He was a sick man. I knew I needed to speak with you, but I consoled myself with the thought that you'd be here when I returned. You weren't, and that was when my life fell apart.'

Cassandra groaned. 'But he must have relented.'

'Oh, yes.' Enrique was sardonic. 'He would never have gone to the trouble of bringing you here if he hadn't felt some responsibility for what had happened.'

'He said you'd entered one of the pens where a bull was being kept. He made it sound as if you'd gone in there deliberately.'

Enrique touched her cheek. 'It was a crazy thing to do.'

'So why did you do it?'

'I was not thinking,' he told her heavily. 'My mind was occupied with other things. I do not believe I did it deliberately, but it is true that since you went away I have had little interest in anything.'

'Oh, Enrique!'

'There,' he said cynically. 'I have laid a guilt trip on you myself. So what are you going to do about it?'

Cassandra looked at his mouth. She was remembering how sensual his mouth was, how delicious it had felt earlier against her skin. 'What do you want me to do about it?' she asked at last, inviting his response, and, with a groan, Enrique sank onto his back against the cushions, taking her with him.

'I can think of many things,' he said, his accent thickening with emotion, and Cassandra was stunned by the sudden strength of his hand at her nape. His mouth found hers with an urgency that brooked no resistance, and with a little cry she surrendered to the magic of his touch...

EPILOGUE

ENRIQUE married Cassandra three weeks later in the small church at Huerta de Tuarega. The whole village turned out for the wedding of *el patrón's* son, and afterwards there was a *fiesta* in the village square.

Despite her happiness, Cassandra couldn't help but compare this wedding with the civil ceremony she and Antonio had shared. This time there had been no question that all the de Montoyas would attend. And, although she doubted Elena de Montoya was overjoyed at the outcome of her husband's interference in his elder son's life, she had had to accept that Enrique loved Cassandra, and only she could make him happy.

Sanchia had attended, too, of course. Along with representatives from all the foremost families in the district, she would have appeared churlish not to do so. Enrique had told Cassandra all about Sanchia: about how quickly she had transferred her attentions to him after Antonio had broken their engagement. He'd also confessed that he and Sanchia had had a passing relationship in recent months. But that as soon as he'd met Cassandra again, he'd had nothing more to do with the other woman.

'Poor Sanchia,' Cassandra had said one evening, a few days after her return to Spain.

She and Enrique had spent the day at the *palacio*, Enrique speaking to his father freely for the first time since his accident, and Cassandra confiding to David that perhaps the hopes he'd had for the future were not so fanciful after all. She'd told him she'd forgiven him for writing to his grandfather. That without his intervention she might never have found happiness at last.

She and Enrique had already talked of getting married, and her son had been in seventh heaven at the thought of having a surrogate father at last. Not that Enrique was a surrogate anything, Cassandra had reflected. But for the present it was kinder to let events proceed at their own pace.

'Why "poor Sanchia"?' Enrique had demanded, taking great pleasure in watching her brush her hair in front of the mirror in his bedroom at La Hacienda. He'd been lounging on the bed, looking much better than when she'd arrived at La Hacienda. The wound on his thigh still looked ugly, but he had started eating again and there had been a trace of healthy colour in his face.

'Why do you think?' she'd countered, putting down the brush and turning towards him. In a cream silk negligee that Elena had lent her, she'd looked unknowingly provocative. 'To lose Antonio was bad enough. To lose you as well must be devastating.'

'If you come here, I will show you exactly how devastating,' he'd told her huskily, stretching out a hand towards her, and Cassandra had gone to him willingly, as captivated by their love as he was.

The days before the wedding had been a magical time. Although Enrique's parents had expected them to return to the *palacio*, both Enrique and Cassandra had preferred to stay at La Hacienda. Ever afterwards, Cassandra would think of it as a pre-honeymoon, and she had been delighted when Enrique decided that the three of them—including David, of course—would live there after they were married.

Cassandra made a beautiful bride. Her dress—a medieval sheath with a cowl neckline and long pointed sleeves—gave her a touching vulnerability. Enrique insisted that she still looked like the virgin she had been when he first knew her, and Cassandra had to confess that there had been no other men since the night David was conceived.

She knew that pleased him. He was still enough of a chauvinist to be glad that she'd known no other man's touch but his. He would deny it, but he was shamelessly possessive where she was concerned.

Henry Skyler had not been surprised when Cassandra sent him her notice. He'd been disappointed she wouldn't be returning to The Bookworm, but hardly surprised. He'd hoped she'd come to see him when she and her husband visited London, and had been kind enough to wish her well.

They were going to the Seychelles for their honeymoon. Enrique said that the islands, set in the Indian ocean, were an ideal place for lovers, and he was determined that they should have at least three weeks to themselves before returning to Tuarega.

Cassandra's father and sisters attended the wedding, too, although as the sister nearest to her in age was pregnant they had decided not to stay long in Spain. Enrique had expressed his delight at their presence, and had persuaded her father to stay on for several days after the wedding so that David could show him the *palacio* and introduce him to the bulls. Mr Scott had demurred at first, but for once Julio de Montoya had been on his best behaviour, due no doubt to his son's influence, and he had endorsed the invitation.

Cassandra was changing for their departure in the bedroom which had been allocated to her at the *palacio* when her new husband came to find her. He entered the room with a distinct and appealing air of satisfaction, closing the door behind him and leaning back against it with undisguised pleasure.

In a lacy bra and panties, Cassandra looked very alluring, and Enrique was not immune to the sensual attractions of her body.

'You look—beautiful,' he said, advancing towards her across the room. He was still wearing the formal morning suit he had worn for their wedding only hours before, but he shed his jacket on the way, unbuttoning his waistcoat with eager fingers. 'Come here.'

'We can't,' she protested, even as her lips responded to the sensuous brush of his. 'Enrique, we don't have time...'

'We will always have time for this,' he insisted huskily, loosening her bra and filling his hands with her breasts. Then, his mouth muffled against her soft flesh, 'Do you want me to stop?'

'Oh, God—no,' she groaned, giving in completely. With his hands cupping her bottom, letting her feel what the pressure of her body was doing to his, she could think of nothing but him. 'But—what if someone comes to find us?'

'We are married,' he reminded her gently. 'We have a son. I do not think anyone can object if I want to make love to my wife.'

If you enjoyed what you just read,
then we've got an offer you can't resist!

Take 2 bestselling love stories FREE!
Plus get a FREE surprise gift!

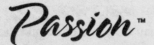
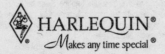

The world's bestselling romance series.

Seduction and Passion Guaranteed!

They're the men who have everything—except a bride…

Wealth, power, charm—what else could a heart-stoppingly
handsome tycoon need? In the GREEK TYCOONS miniseries
you have already been introduced to some gorgeous Greek
multimillionaires who are in need of wives.

Now it's the turn of favorite Presents author

Helen Brooks,

with her attention-grabbing romance

THE GREEK TYCOON'S BRIDE

Harlequin Presents #2255
Available in June

This tycoon has met his match, and he's decided he *has* to
have her…*whatever* that takes!

Pick up a Harlequin Presents® novel and you will
enter a world of spine-tingling passion and
provocative, tantalizing romance!

Available wherever Harlequin books are sold.

Coming Next Month

HARLEQUIN *Presents*

THE BEST HAS JUST GOTTEN BETTER!

#2253 THE ARRANGED MARRIAGE Emma Darcy
Alex King is the eldest grandson of a prestigious family—and it's his duty to expand the King empire. He must find a bride and then father a son. Alex thinks he's made the right choice, so why is his grandmother so eager to change his mind?

#2254 THE SHEIKH'S CHOSEN WIFE Michelle Reid
Leona misses her arrogant, passionate husband, Sheikh Hassan ben Al-Qadim, very much. She'd left him after she'd been unable to give him the heir he needed. But a year later Hassan tricks her into returning....

#2255 THE GREEK TYCOON'S BRIDE Helen Brooks
Andreas Karydis had women falling at his feet, so Sophy was determined not be another notch in his bedpost. But he doesn't want her as his mistress—he wants her as his English bride!

#2256 THE MISTRESS SCANDAL Kim Lawrence
Ally didn't regret her one night of passion with Gabe MacAllister and had never forgotten it. She was reminded every time she looked at her baby son. Then three years later, Ally is stunned to discover that Gabe is the brother of her sister's new fiancé!

#2257 EXPECTING HIS BABY Sandra Field
Lise knew all about ruthless airline tycoon Judd Harwood—but he needed a nanny for his daughter, Emmy, and against her better judgment Lise took the job. She never intended to spend a night of blazing passion in his bed!

#2258 THE PLAYBOY'S PROPOSAL Amanda Browning
Joel Kendrick was the sexiest man Kathryn had ever met. Never one to refuse a challenge, she flirted back when Joel flirted with her! But flirting turned to desire on Joel's part—and true love on Kathryn's....

HPCNM0502